THE MYSTERIOUS IMAGE

THE MYSTERIOUS IMAGE

by
Carolyn Keene

Illustrated by
Paul Frame

WANDERER BOOKS
Published by Simon & Schuster, Inc., New York

Published by WANDERER BOOKS
A Division of Simon & Schuster, Inc.
Simon & Schuster Building
1230 Avenue of the Americas
New York, New York 10020

Manufactured in the United States of America
10 9 8 7 6 5 4 3 2

NANCY DREW and NANCY DREW MYSTERY STORIES
are trademarks of Stratemeyer Syndicate,
registered in the United States Patent
and Trademark Office

WANDERER and colophon are registered trademarks of
Simon & Schuster, Inc.

Library of Congress Cataloging in Publication Data

Keene, Carolyn.
The mysterious image.

(Nancy Drew mystery stories ; 74)
Summary: Nancy sets out to locate a kidnapped actress
and to clear one of her father's clients, a renowned
photographer, accused of stealing ideas for his images.
[1. Mystery and detective stories] I. Frame, Paul,
1913-   ill. II. Title. III. Series: Keene, Carolyn. Nancy
Drew mystery stories ; 74.
PZ7.K23Nan no. 74   [Fic]   83-16898
ISBN 0-671-49738-3
ISBN 0-671-49737-5 (pbk.)

Contents

1

Disappearing Act

"Oh, Dad, look!" exclaimed Nancy Drew. "Isn't this striking?"

As she nibbled on some toast, the young detective leafed through a magazine that had arrived in the morning mail. She slid it across the breakfast table and pointed to a full-page advertisement that had caught her eye.

The photographic layout showed a bronze African idol with a diamond and emerald necklace. The gems seemed to glow with even more fiery radiance by contrast with the eerie-looking figure.

Nancy's father, Attorney Carson Drew, nodded. "Beautiful—a very artistic ad! I happen to know this is the work of Dallas Curry."

"That famous photographer who's a friend of yours?" Nancy queried.

"Yes—and not only a friend, but a client. I'm about to defend him in a lawsuit."

"For goodness sake, Dad! Whatever for?"

"Believe it or not, he's accused of *copying* other people's work—of stealing their ideas."

Nancy was startled. "But that's incredible! Dallas Curry is world-famous, isn't he? Why on earth would he want to pirate someone else's work?"

Mr. Drew nodded grimly. "Good question. The whole thing doesn't make sense. Dallas Curry has become the most highly paid advertising photographer in America just because he creates such unique images—like this one of the African idol with a necklace that you've just shown me. Yet, apparently he copied three separate layouts that were shot by other photographers for other ad agencies. He himself can't explain it."

"Have you seen the advertisements, Dad?"

"Yes, and I'll have to admit the similarity seems too great to be mere coincidence." The distinguished trial lawyer sighed and shook his head. "It's really quite a mystery, Nancy. I may need your help in handling the case."

Nancy's blue eyes sparkled with interest at

the challenge. "Sounds fascinating! I'd love to help if I can."

The strawberry-blonde detective had already solved a number of baffling mysteries, and her skill at sleuthing had made the name of Nancy Drew well known far beyond her hometown of River Heights.

"Who exactly is suing Mr. Curry?" she inquired. "The other photographers?"

"No, a firm called Marc Joplin, Incorporated—one of the three advertising agencies that claim their ads were copied," replied Mr. Drew. "Recently they did one for a cosmetic company that ran in *Flair* magazine. It featured a picture of flowers with models' faces on the flower blossoms. A week or so later, an ad for a rival cosmetic company appeared in another magazine with exactly the same layout, this one photographed by Dallas Curry!"

Nancy was astounded. Before she could comment, the telephone rang. Knowing that their housekeeper, Hannah Gruen, was busy in the kitchen, she rose from the table. "Excuse me, while I answer that."

Nancy hurried out to the front hall. The caller was her old friend, Police Chief McGinnis. "Sorry to bother you so early on a Monday morning, Nancy, but a situation has come up where a private detective would come in mighty handy. How would you like to investigate a disappearance?"

Nancy chuckled. Apparently today was her morning for mysteries—and this one sounded intriguing! "Glad to, Chief. Who disappeared?"

"A young actress named Clare Grant. Ever heard of her?"

"Why, yes. Didn't she star in a Broadway play a while back? And I believe I read in the paper that she was staying in River Heights this summer."

"Right on both counts, Nancy. Anyhow, she seems to have vanished overnight, and a friend of hers is raising quite a fuss about it."

"Who's the friend?" asked Nancy.

"A young lady named Pamela Kane, who just flew in from California. She's demanding that we launch a full investigation right away, but as you know, the police can't legally take any action until a person has been missing for at least twenty-four hours. So I suggested that Miss Kane put the case in your hands."

Chief McGinnis explained that Clare Grant had been staying at the home of friends on Possum Road. Nancy jotted down the address and promised to go there at once.

Returning to the dining room, she told her father about the call and apologized for having to break off their conversation.

"That's all right, my dear," said Carson Drew, setting down his coffee cup and dabbing his mouth with a napkin. "I've an early appointment, so I must be running along. We'll talk more about the Curry case later on."

Soon after her father left the house, Nancy was backing her sleek blue sports car out of the garage. Possum Road ran eastward out of town into a pleasant, rolling green area of wealthy estates. Most of them were on the north side of the road. The opposite side, being rugged and hilly, was still mostly undeveloped.

Chief McGinnis had told Nancy that the house where Clare Grant had been spending the summer was owned by a Mr. and Mrs. Fyfe, a couple who were vacationing in Europe. During the owners' absence, both their guest and the property were being looked after by their cook and housekeeper, Mrs. Barrow.

Presently Nancy turned up a graveled drive and stopped in front of the large, white chateau-style house. In response to her ring, the door was opened by a middle-aged woman in a gray, white-collared servant's uniform. Evidently this was Mrs. Barrow.

"Miss Drew?" she said to Nancy. "Please come in. Detective Hoyt is expecting you."

She led the way to the drawing room, where the plainclothes police officer was speaking to a worried-looking young woman with fluffy blonde hair. Her brown eyes peered out anxiously at the world through pearl-rimmed pixie glasses.

"Hi, Nancy," said Detective Hoyt. "This is Miss Pamela Kane. She's a friend of Clare Grant, the young lady who seems to be missing."

"She *is* missing. There's no doubt about it!" Pamela Kane choked back a sob. Her eyes were red-rimmed from weeping, and her fingers were twisting and kneading a damp hanky. "That's why I'm so glad you're here, Nancy. I've heard ever so much about you! I just pray you can find Clare before it's too late. I'm terribly afraid something awful's happened to her!"

"Let's hope you're wrong, but I'll certainly do my best," Nancy promised. When they were all seated, she went on, "Please tell me how you discovered your friend's disappearance."

The story came out in snatches with Pamela, Detective Hoyt, and the housekeeper all helping to fill Nancy in. The Fyfes, she learned, had generously told their guest to treat the house as her own while they were gone. Accordingly, on Sunday evening, Clare Grant told Mrs. Barrow that she was expecting a friend—Pamela Kane—to join her the next morning.

Soon after 8:00 A.M., Pamela had arrived by taxi from the airport. Mrs. Barrow had answered the door and let her in. But when she went to inform Clare Grant of her friend's arrival, Clare's room was empty. Since then, the whole house had been searched with no result. The young actress had disappeared! Finally Mrs. Barrow called the police.

"Any sign of a struggle?" asked Nancy.

Detective Hoyt shook his head. "None, although her bedroom window was wide open."

"But she told me on the phone that she'd been receiving threats!" Pamela Kane cut in. "That's partly why I made the trip East—because she sounded so worried and fearful."

"Did Clare tell you who made the threats?" Nancy inquired.

"No, she even seemed afraid to talk about it. I was hoping that after I got here, I could persuade her to confide in me—but as you see, I came too late!" Pamela's lips trembled. She dabbed her nose with her hanky and seemed on the verge of bursting into tears again.

"Could I see Clare's room?" Nancy murmured hastily, changing the subject.

"Of course." The housekeeper rose from her chair. "Let me show you the way."

The bedroom—which was in the rear of the house, on the first floor—was large and comfortably furnished. The coverlet had been thrown back, and the bed looked as if it had been slept in.

The room had two windows with green silken draperies. The one nearest the bed was wide open. "Was this how you found it?" Nancy asked and pointed.

"Yes." Mrs. Barrow said that most of the windows were kept closed, since the house was air conditioned. "But Miss Grant was quite a fresh-air fiend," she added with a wan smile. "She liked to sleep with her window open."

"No screen?"

"There was one, but it got damaged on Saturday, so I called our handyman to have it fixed. But Miss Grant opened her window at night even while it was gone. I guess she didn't mind the insects."

Nancy gazed out at the rear grounds. The well-tended lawn and shrubbery were bordered by a dense, wild grove of trees. "How far back do those woods extend?" she wondered aloud.

"Almost a mile," Detective Hoyt replied.

"They run in back of all the houses on this side of Possum Road."

Nancy turned to the housekeeper again. "When was the last time you spoke to Clare Grant?"

Mrs. Barrow said she had received a call from Clare on the house phone shortly after 1:30 A.M. "She sounded a bit disturbed."

"What about?"

"She thought she'd heard noises out back. In fact, she even thought she might have glimpsed someone skulking out there."

Nancy asked, "Did you call the police?"

"No, though I offered to. First I switched on the ground lights. That would have caught any prowler by surprise, because they light up the whole yard. But we could see there was nobody out there. I guess that reassured her, because then when I offered to phone the police, she said not to bother."

"The lights wouldn't *prove* there was no prowler," Pamela Kane argued. "He might have ducked behind some shrubbery."

"But at any rate you heard nothing further from Miss Grant after that one call?" Nancy asked Mrs. Barrow.

"That's right," the housekeeper said and nodded.

"So presumably," Nancy mused, "she must

have disappeared sometime between . . . well, say about 2:00 A.M. and 8:00 A.M."

"Clare certainly wouldn't just walk off without telling anybody," said Pamela. "And she wouldn't leave the window that wide open just for fresh air, either."

"Are any of her things missing?" asked Nancy.

"Not as far as I can tell," said Mrs. Barrow.

"Have the woods been searched?"

The detective shook his head. "Not yet."

"Then let's look right now," Nancy proposed.

The housekeeper remained behind while Nancy, Pamela, and the police officer started out toward the woods. They had barely entered the first fringe of trees when Nancy saw a shiny scrap of paper clinging to a patch of underbrush. She picked it up and was startled to see that it bore a picture of a girl's face.

Pamela cried out excitedly, *"That's Clare!"*

2

A Puzzling Trail

"It's a piece of a photograph," said Detective Hoyt. He shot a frowning glance at Nancy.

Both were troubled by the same thoughts. Why had a picture of the actress been torn up, and who had dropped the fragment of her photo in the woods?

"Oh, Nancy, I don't like the looks of this!" wailed Pamela Kane. "Maybe whoever broke into Clare's room last night tore up her picture in a rage! What do you suppose has happened to her?"

"Come on, we'll find out," Nancy said soothingly, putting her arm around the trembling woman. "Meanwhile, don't jump to any conclusions."

"That's good advice," said Detective Hoyt.

"Now let's spread out and keep our eyes open. And we'd better watch out for poison ivy, too!"

Pushing on through the woods became increasingly difficult. The trees grew closer together, casting deeper shadows. The underbrush was also thicker. Soon another fragment of the torn picture was found by Detective Hoyt. Then Nancy spotted another.

Bit by bit, as the three worked their way through the cool, damp woods, they picked up additional pieces until they were able to form a general impression of the whole photograph.

To their amazement, it showed Clare Grant posed like the Statue of Liberty, with torch and book, atop a marble column! She was wearing a diamond tiara and clad in a stunning evening gown of white silk, woven with glittering metallic threads.

The police officer scratched his head and looked up at his two companions with a puzzled grin. "What's with this Statue of Liberty bit? Is it some kind of joke?"

"No, wait! I recognize it now!" exclaimed Nancy. "This was an advertising layout that Clare Grant modeled for. I remember seeing it in a magazine about a year ago. It was a department store ad featuring some fashion designer's line of evening wear."

"Okay, if you say so, Nancy," Detective Hoyt

commented somewhat uncertainly. "But I'd sure like to know how all these pieces got scattered through the woods."

"So would I!" declared Pamela in a fervently anxious voice.

"Let's be patient," said Nancy. "I'm sure we can work out the answer eventually if we try hard enough."

The trail of the torn photo finally led them out of the woods into a big clearing. The vegetation underfoot was sparse in this area, and the ground was still mushy and soft from the heavy rains that had drenched River Heights over the weekend.

Here and there, a few confused footprints were visible—evidently made by a man's shoes, and leading both to and from the edge of the clearing—but for the most part they seemed to be purposely scattered over rocks and pebbles, to avoid leaving any clear traces.

"I don't see any female footprints," Detective Hoyt remarked.

"He could have been *carrying* Clare," Pamela pointed out.

If so, Nancy reflected, it might explain why the few prints that were visible seemed to have been pressed into the mud so deeply. But she refrained from saying so aloud in order to avoid frightening Pamela still more. After all, the prints might simply have been made by a person of heavy build.

In the center of the clearing was a large excavation—obviously an old, abandoned rock quarry. "Oh-h-h!" Pamela wailed again and stumbled toward the edge of the crater to peer down into its depths. But the excavation was empty, with little or no residue of water from the recent storm.

The ground immediately surrounding the crater was strewn with too much gravel and broken rock to show any footprints. Nancy began walking around the quarry, searching for clues, with Pamela close at her heels, while Detective Hoyt circled it in the opposite direction.

When they met on the opposite side of the quarry, they found themselves looking at clear tire tracks in the mushy ground.

Nancy studied the heavily ridged tread marks. "Those are the kind of tire treads that a four-wheel-drive vehicle would have, aren't they, Detective Hoyt?"

"Right you are, Nancy. Obviously an ATV was driven here. You know—an all-terrain, or off-the-road, vehicle, the kind that can be driven over any ground," the detective observed.

The tire tracks led from the quarry to an old,

deeply rutted cinder path, which seemed to meander through the woods at a roughly northwesterly slant. Although there was no hope of making out the tire tracks on the cindered trail, it seemed obvious that the mystery vehicle had traveled in a direction opposite to the Fyfes' house.

"Do you know where this cindered path leads to?" Nancy asked Hoyt.

"Yes, I do. It connects up with Highway 19 on the other side of the woods, about a mile from here. And the opposite end joins Possum Road a little way east of the Fyfes' house."

After pondering for a few moments, Nancy said, "Well, I think we've done all we can here for now." And pushing her red-gold hair back from her face, the teenager turned and led the way back through the woods toward the house.

Stepping through a border of forsythias and rhododendrons, they finally reached the lawn and fragrant gardens at the rear of the Fyfes' estate.

Detective Hoyt bent down to brush the mud off his trouser cuffs, then as he straightened up said, "Don't worry too much, Miss Kane. Your friend hasn't been gone very long and maybe she'll soon be back. But I'll be in touch. Right now I'd better be getting back to headquarters."

When he had gone, Nancy pointed to a group of white garden furniture on a tiled patio. "Why don't we sit down over there, and you can help by telling me more about Clare Grant."

When they were seated, Pamela Kane said hesitantly, "I'd like to ask the housekeeper to bring you some refreshment, Nancy, but I'm a little unsure about whether I should stay here or exactly what I should do until Clare comes back."

"I'm sure you're welcome to stay here until your friend returns," Nancy replied sympathetically. "After all, Clare Grant did invite you here as her guest. And she may come back at any moment."

"I certainly hope so," Pamela said, not very confidently, clasping and unclasping her hands.

"What can you tell me about Clare?" said Nancy, encouraging her to talk. "Her career might be a good place to start."

"Clare was stagestruck; that's the only word for it." Pamela Kane smiled reminiscently.

"When she finished college out in the Midwest, she came straight to Broadway. And was she lucky! She landed a part almost immediately and scored an instant hit! It was in a play called *The Mandrake Root*."

Nancy nodded. "Yes, I remember."

Pamela's smile faded as she went on, "Since then, Clare hasn't been quite so lucky. After *The Mandrake Root*, she got a part in another play, but it flopped—opened and closed in one week, in fact! Then she tried the movies and got a couple of small film roles out in Hollywood. That's where I met her."

"You're an actress, too?" Nancy asked.

"Well, hopefully—but not very successful yet. Anyway, Clare came back East in order to clinch the lead role in a play called *Perfect Strangers*. It's due to open this fall. She's just right for the part, too—and she wants it so badly! That's why I'm sure she must have been kidnapped, Nancy. Why would she disappear now, just when her career's about to get another boost?"

Once again Pamela Kane began to wring her hands nervously as she added, "Oh, there must be *something* we can do!"

"You can rest assured that I'll do my very best to find her, Pam," Nancy promised. "In the meantime, the best way you can help is by staying here near the phone, in case Clare calls or anyone else has some information about her."

24

Nancy patted Pamela's hand reassuringly and stood up.

"Oh, do you mean her kidnapper might call, demanding ransom?" Pamela asked in a quavering voice.

"Not necessarily. The main thing is to keep calm. Just remember, we haven't seen any evidence of violence. But I'll get busy, and I'll keep you informed," Nancy added as they started around the house toward her car, parked on the front drive.

The young detective puzzled over the case of the missing actress as she drove home along tree-shaded Possum Road.

When Nancy walked into the cool, pleasant hallway of the Drew home, Hannah Gruen emerged from the kitchen. The motherly housekeeper had taken care of Nancy ever since Mrs. Drew had died when her daughter was a tot of three. "Oh, Nancy," Hannah greeted her with a smile, "your father phoned here just a few minutes ago and wants you to call him at his office."

"Okay, Hannah, thanks." Nancy headed for the telephone. But before she could pick it up, the front doorbell chimed. "I'll get that," she added.

When she opened the door, a mailman was

standing on the porch. "Special delivery for Miss Nancy Drew."

"I'm Nancy Drew," she replied.

He thrust a small, brown-paper-wrapped package into her hands, then turned and hurried back down the porch steps toward his mail truck.

Nancy examined the package curiously. It bore no return address or sender's name. Repressing a smile from her own suspicions about it, she held the package up to her ear and listened for a moment, then shook it a little. But neither precaution gave her any clue to its contents.

Nancy unwrapped the package carefully. Inside was a video cassette, of the kind used on a home video recorder.

But it, too, bore no title or identifying label!

3

An Odd Dislike

Intrigued, Nancy stared at the cassette. Her first impulse was to run to the video recorder and play the tape. But remembering that she was to call her father at his office, she set the cassette down on the hall table, picked up the telephone, and dialed his office number.

Carson Drew's efficient, pleasant-voiced secretary, Miss Hanson, answered.

"Hi! This is Nancy returning Dad's call," the teenager told her.

"Oh, Nancy. I'm sorry, you just missed him. Your father had to go to the courthouse. But he asked me to tell you that he'll be meeting Dallas Curry for lunch at one-thirty, and he'd like you to join them. The restaurant is the Fisherman's Net. Do you know where it is?"

"Yes, I've lunched there with Dad before. Thanks for letting me know," Nancy said and hung up.

Going into the living room, she eagerly switched on the television set and slipped the cassette into the video recorder. Then she settled herself into an easy chair facing the screen and watched what was on the tape.

To her surprise, a video scene appeared, accompanied by the throbbing beat of a famous rock group and the voice of their lead singer. The number played for several minutes and was followed, one after another, by a series of similar rock videos. But there was no explanation of the gift.

Nancy was baffled. Who on earth could have sent it? she wondered. One of her girl friends, perhaps Bess Marvin or George Fayne, or her favorite date, Ned Nickerson? But they would know that while Nancy enjoyed music, both classical and pop, she wasn't really a great rock fan. So maybe the cassette had been sent to her simply as a joke.

But if so, by whom?

Oh well, it's not really important, Nancy decided with a sigh. She rose from the comfortable wing chair and went upstairs to shower and change into a simple, sleeveless blue linen dress. After brushing her hair, she picked up a white straw handbag, started downstairs again, and, with a called-out good-bye to Hannah, went back out to her car.

As she drove to the restaurant in the downtown section of River Heights, Nancy found herself thinking of her father's law client whom she was about to meet. Beyond the basic facts that he was a world-famous photographer, owned a showplace home in River Heights, and was a friend of her father's, she really knew very little about Dallas Curry.

Yet, oddly, Nancy realized that her attitude toward him was already faintly tinged with dislike, and that she was not looking forward to lunch. Was it because of the accusations that had been made against Curry? It must be. What other reason was there?

"But that's silly," Nancy chided herself. "I certainly know enough, from all Dad has taught me, never to prejudge a case!"

Minutes later, Nancy parked her car in a lot near the Fisherman's Net. Upon entering the restaurant, Nancy looked around and saw her father seated at a table with a casually but well-dressed younger man. Carson Drew waved to her, and as she joined them, they both smiled and rose to greet her.

"Ah, Nancy, I'd like you to meet Dallas Curry," said the tall, broad-shouldered attorney. "Dallas, this is my daughter, Nancy."

"A pleasure, Nancy. I've heard a great deal about you," Dallas said with a smile.

"You're not exactly unknown yourself," she twinkled back.

Dallas Curry was a lean, vigorous-looking man in his late thirties, with a handsome, deeply tanned face and a shock of long, dark chestnut hair that was thinning at the temples.

Sitting down, they studied their menus and ordered from the assortment of seafood specialties, then sat back and began chatting while they waited to be served.

As the lunch progressed, Nancy had to admit that she was enjoying herself, in spite of her somewhat negative feelings at the outset. The lobster was delicious, and Dallas Curry proved to be an entertaining conversationalist. He was widely traveled and had photographed news and other events in almost every country in the world.

She learned that he had first made a name as a freelance war photographer. Later he had won acclaim as a staff photographer for *Glance* magazine, shooting picture stories on everything from chemical plants to rock musicians. His photos had been collected, published, and exhibited in art galleries and museums.

While he was telling Nancy and Carson Drew

amusing stories of his experiences, Nancy remembered her father saying that Dallas Curry was the most talented, highly paid advertising photographer in the business. Once again she wondered, what motive could such a man possibly have for copying someone else's work?

In Mr. Drew's own words, the whole thing just didn't make sense!

After coffee, the three left the restaurant and walked to Carson Drew's law office to discuss the unpleasant charges made against his client.

"Dallas, you may have read or heard about some of the baffling mysteries Nancy has solved," the lawyer began.

"I have, indeed. If she can get to the bottom of this crazy mess I've become involved in, I'll be more grateful than I can say. In fact," the photographer went on, "now that I've met you, Nancy, I really believe that if anyone can help me, you can. I've always trusted to instinct in my own work, you see, and right now—well, don't ask me why, but somehow I've a feeling that your combination of brains and charm may be just what's needed to clear up this mystery."

"Thank you." The titian-blonde teenager smiled back at him. "I'll certainly do my best."

"Now then," said Mr. Drew, "let's backtrack a bit for Nancy's sake and go over some of the information you've already given me. These charges against you involve three different photographic assignments and three different advertising agencies, is that right?"

"Yes, and so help me, the more I think about all this, the weirder it seems! It almost makes me wonder if I'm losing my mind!"

As he spoke, Curry ran his fingers distractedly through his hair. For a moment, Nancy couldn't help pitying the famed photographer as his haggard expression betrayed the worry and confusion that were preying on his mind.

"I believe the first instance was a fashion ad of some sort," Mr. Drew prompted him.

Dallas Curry nodded. "Right. I was hired to shoot a high-fashion layout for a department store." Reaching into his leather portfolio, he pulled out a large, glossy reproduction of the advertisement and laid it on the lawyer's desk. "This was scheduled to appear in *Milady* magazine. But less than a week before that particular issue came out, another ad—almost exactly like this—appeared in another magazine."

As she looked at the eye-catching layout, Nancy gasped. It featured the same photograph of Clare Grant that she and Detective Hoyt and Pamela Kane had found torn and scattered in the woods that morning!

4

Picture Snapper

Though startled, Nancy decided not to interrupt Dallas Curry's story. He was already taking a magazine called *Nightlife* out of his portfolio.

Curry opened the magazine to a full-color advertisement. Pictorially, it was almost an exact duplicate of the layout he had just shown them! Nancy could hardly believe her eyes. This, too, showed a fashion model posed like the Statue of Liberty atop a marble column. The only difference was that she was wearing a beautiful white fur coat rather than a white evening gown.

"Amazing!" murmured Carson Drew. "Do you know exactly when this one was photographed?"

Dallas Curry shook his head glumly. "No, I've never been able to pin that down. All that mattered was that it got published before mine."

"Was there any accusation of copying?" Nancy asked.

"Not at that time. Of course it caused a lot of talk in advertising circles, and it was mighty embarrassing for me. But I guess most people were willing to put it down to coincidence. But now let me show you what happened next."

Again Curry pulled a large, colorful ad layout from his portfolio. This one showed several knights in armor seated with raised flagons at a round dining-room table of lustrous mahogany. The picture was captioned: *Styled for the Ages!*

"About ten days before this was published in *Modern Life* magazine," Curry went on, "a similar ad appeared in *Decor* magazine."

He took out the latter and opened it to the advertisement in question. This, too, featured a round table and knights, posed almost identically to those in Curry's layout, and was headed: *Our Furniture Never Goes Out of Fashion!*

"This case of duplication," said Curry, "occurred about two or three months after the first instance that I just showed you concerning the Statue of Liberty layout."

"Same photographer?" asked Nancy.

"No, a different photographer and a different ad agency. But this one didn't get by so easily. The rival agent went to the Advertising Council and charged the agency I was working for with ethical misconduct. In plain English, they claimed their ad had been copied," Curry said in a bitter voice. "As it turned out, the dispute was settled quietly—which didn't help me. By now my reputation was really hurting. Twice in a row seemed a little too much to be called a coincidence. A good many people were ready to believe that I'd deliberately stolen someone else's idea. And my problems *still* weren't over!"

Once again the famed photographer took out an example of his work and an almost identical advertisement that had appeared before his own was published. This was the instance that Mr. Drew had told Nancy about at the breakfast table—a cosmetics ad featuring models' faces superimposed on flowers.

"I shot mine early this spring," said Curry, "but the other was published two weeks before mine, in a different magazine."

Nancy and her father exchanged baffled glances.

"And this is the one that caused the lawsuit?" the girl inquired.

"Right." Curry nodded and rose abruptly to begin pacing about the lawyer's office. "Mind you, I don't blame the other agency a bit. It does look like outright copying—a plain case of artistic theft." He punched his fist into his open palm, adding, "And I'm at a total loss to explain it!"

"Let me just ask this for the record," said Mr. Drew cautiously. "You're quite sure you never saw those other ads while they were being prepared?"

"I'm absolutely certain of it," declared Curry. "As far as I'm concerned, these layouts of mine are just as original as anything else I've ever done. And they were created amid the usual secrecy that surrounds every new advertising campaign."

"Did any of the three instances involve the same photographer or the same ad agency?" asked Nancy.

Again Curry shook his head. "No, each of the other three ads was done by a different agency and a different photographer. So if you're thinking of some carefully laid plot against me, I'd say it's out of the question."

Nancy sighed and frowned thoughtfully. "You certainly do have a mystery on your hands, Mr. Curry. I'll do my best to help solve it, but beyond that, I'd better not promise any-thing."

Nancy took out a pen and notebook from her handbag and jotted down the names and addresses of all the parties involved. Then she told Curry about finding the torn-up photo modeled by Clare Grant. Curry was astonished and concerned to learn that the young actress had disappeared.

"How well did you know her?" Nancy asked.

"I met her not long before her Broadway debut," the photographer replied. "*Glance* magazine assigned me to shoot a picture story about a typical young Broadway hopeful. A theatrical agent suggested Clare, and she seemed perfect for the kind of story *Glance* wanted. The editor used one of my shots of her on the cover that week, and it drew a lot of fan mail. As a matter of fact, that exposure helped win Clare her first Broadway role."

"In *The Mandrake Root*," Nancy recalled.

"Yes ... which turned into a big hit, as you probably know. And ever since then, Clare and I have been friends."

"How did you happen to choose her for that Statue of Liberty evening-gown layout?"

Dallas Curry shrugged. "She's a beautiful girl. I knew she'd photograph well. Also, I knew she was 'in between jobs' at the time, as actors say, so I figured she could use the money."

The young sleuth smiled encouragingly. "Let's hope I can turn up some clues that will help Dad win your case."

Curry summoned up a rueful smile. "I'm not only hoping so, Nancy—I'm counting on it!"

She crossed her fingers. "In the meantime, I'll leave you two to discuss the legal angles."

As Nancy left the building in which her father's law office was located, she glimpsed a tall, lanky young man with bleached blond hair and an expensive-looking camera slung around his neck.

Nancy raised her brow thoughtfully. Haven't I seen him somewhere before? she wondered. And quite recently, too, it seemed. Why else would he look so familiar?

She paused to gaze at a shop window—and suddenly the answer came to her. She had noticed him at the Fisherman's Net just an hour or so earlier. He had been sitting not far from their table as she lunched with her father and Dallas Curry.

Curious at seeing the same person again so soon, Nancy turned to glance again at the blond young man. To her amazement, his camera was now raised in front of his face. *He was snapping a picture of her!*

Nancy had unraveled too many mysteries and had helped her father in too many lawsuits to be taken by surprise. Her suspicions were instantly aroused.

"I'd better find out what he's up to!" she whispered to herself.

As she headed toward him, her heels tapping sharply on the pavement, the young man turned and sprinted away. Nancy pursued him to the next block, where she saw him jump into a yellow convertible and gun the engine.

Luckily the parking lot where she'd left her own car was in the same block. As the young man drove out into the stream of traffic, Nancy kept on running. Moments later her blue sports car was heading out of the lot. A distant red traffic light, which had temporarily stopped the fugitive cameraman, was just now turning green.

Nancy thrust her left hand out the window, handing her parking ticket and money to the lot attendant. Then, without waiting for change, she zoomed out into the street!

The yellow convertible was no longer in sight. But by stepping on the accelerator as hard as she dared, and by maneuvering deftly from one lane to another, she gradually brought the car into view.

Nancy permitted herself a faint smile of triumph. The furtive shutter-snapper was not going to get away from her as easily as he thought!

Her smile faded several blocks later as the avenue ahead took a sharp turn to the right. Within moments her quarry was out of sight again—which meant if he left Central Avenue before she got him back in view, she would be unable to tell which way he had gone!

Thinking fast, Nancy turned right to race down a slanting side street. With luck, the shortcut might bring her back to the avenue soon enough to glimpse him again before he disappeared completely.

But just as she swung her steering wheel, a man stepped out from the curb, waving at her. Nancy caught her breath and jammed on the brakes hard to avoid hitting him!

5

Clue Search

Thank heavens these brakes are good! thought Nancy. Her hands were shaking and her heart was jumping as the car stopped with a screech of tires.

The pedestrian she had seen out of the corner of her eye just in the nick of time was now coming up to the car door. Nancy gasped in relief as she recognized her boyfriend, Ned Nickerson. He opened the car door and swiftly slid in beside her.

"Sorry I scared us both so, Nancy!" the handsome college student apologized with a grin. "When I saw you and stepped off the curb to flag you down, I didn't expect you to turn so suddenly."

"I'm sorry too, Ned." Nancy reached out for a moment to squeeze his hand before starting up again. Horns were already honking behind her. "The turn was a spur-of-the-moment decision," she explained while swerving onto the side street. "I was tailing a yellow convertible in connection with a case I'm working on, but I lost sight of it around that bend in Central Avenue. So I thought if I took a shortcut, I might have a better chance of picking it up again."

"Don't let me stop you!" Ned chuckled, entering into the spirit of the case. "We'll both keep our eyes peeled."

As it turned out, however, precious moments had been lost, and the quarry was too far out of range to be overtaken. After cutting back onto Central Avenue, Nancy continued the pursuit for another half-dozen blocks. But neither she nor Ned was able to glimpse the blond picture-snapper in his convertible.

"Oh well, if he's really important to the case, I'll probably see him again," Nancy said philosophically.

"What I *do* see up ahead is an ice cream parlor," said Ned. "I suggest we stop in and console ourselves with a soda or milk shake. How about it?"

"Sounds good to me." Nancy laughed as she pulled over to the curb and parked.

After they were seated and had ordered, Ned remarked, "It was a lucky break spotting you, Nancy. Telepathy maybe! I called your house a little while ago, but Hannah said you'd gone out. I wanted to invite you to dinner tonight. Can you make it?"

"Oh, I'd love that, Ned. I'm so glad you're home again," Nancy replied enthusiastically.

It was summer vacation time for Ned Nickerson, who attended Emerson College. "I've just been offered a summer job in an advertising agency, by the way," he went on, "but I'm not sure yet whether I want to take it. It involves market research ... you know, finding out whether or not people will buy a certain product, and what it takes to convince them."

"Sounds interesting. I'm into advertising myself on this latest mystery I'm trying to solve." While they were pursuing the yellow convertible, Nancy had already told Ned some of the details about the weird duplication of magazine ads that had plagued Dallas Curry. Neither could guess how the lanky blond cameraman might fit into the case.

As they sipped their milk shakes, Nancy described some of the unusual photographic layouts that Curry was accused of copying. The conversation then turned to television commercials. Suddenly Nancy remembered the mysterious video cassette that had been sent to her. She told Ned about it and added, "You didn't send it to me, did you?"

"No, I know you aren't fond of rock music, Nancy," he said. "Maybe George or Bess did it as a joke."

She nodded. "I'll ask them."

When they had finished their shakes, Nancy and Ned walked back to her blue sports car. "Can I drop you anywhere, Ned?"

"Well, as a matter of fact, the ad agency that offered me a job is located just a couple of blocks from here." The husky six-footer glanced at his watch. "They asked me to come in for a three-o'clock interview, so I could use a lift there, if you're heading toward Park Street."

Nancy smiled. "Wherever you say, sir!"

A few minutes later she stopped to let him off. "Thanks. See you tonight!" he waved before walking into the office building.

Nancy drove home and was delighted to find Bess Marvin and George Fayne waiting for her. Though cousins, the two girls were strikingly different in looks. Bess was blonde and slightly plump, while George was a slim, athletic girl with short, dark hair.

"The very two people I wanted to see!" Nancy cried on discovering them in the living room.

"Well, it's nice to know we're wanted."
George said and winked at Bess.

"Yes, but for what?" Her cousin finished the
candy bar she'd been nibbling on and wadded
up the wrapper.

"For one thing, to ask you both a question,"
Nancy replied. "Did either of you send me a
video cassette?"

She knew they hadn't when she saw their
puzzled faces, even before they shook their
heads no. Nancy told them how the package
had arrived with no sender's name or address
and how, when she played the cassette on the
video recorder, the tape had proved to contain a
series of rock-music videos.

"Gee, that's odd," George murmured.

"It certainly is," Bess agreed. "Can we see it,
Nancy?"

"Oh, I'll play it for you later—that's a promise. But first, will you do me a favor and keep
me company on a walk . . . please?"

"Sure, I'd enjoy a little exercise," said
George.

Bess, however, emitted a doleful groan. "Oh,
no-o-o! If 'walk' is a polite name for a hike,
count me out."

"Pretty please?" asked Nancy.

At this point, George cut in firmly, "Listen,
my little butterball of a cousin. You need the

exercise more than either of us do. So come on, be a sport!"

Bess was finally persuaded. Nancy quickly changed into loafers and jeans. Then the three girls got into Nancy's car and started eastward out of town.

"What's this all about, Nancy?" George inquired, suspecting a mystery.

As she drove along Possum Road, Nancy told her two chums about the strange disappearance of Clare Grant. She also pointed out, in passing the white chateau-style home of the Fyfes, where the young actress had been staying just before she vanished.

Presently Nancy stopped at a point where a cinder path from the woods cut into Possum Road. "This is one end of the path that slants by that quarry I told you about," Nancy explained. "I'd like to follow it all the way through the woods to Highway 19 and look for clues."

Despite her lack of enthusiasm for hiking, even Bess was excited at the prospect. "Oh, it would be thrilling," she breathed, "if we found some clue that enabled you to nab her kidnappers, Nancy!"

"It sure would . . . if she was kidnapped," George added more cautiously.

"Yes, that's an important question," Nancy

agreed. "Either way, it's a puzzling situation. If Clare Grant *was* kidnapped, why didn't she call for help or put up a struggle? But on the other hand, why would she go off on her own accord in the middle of the night just when she was expecting a friend to come and visit her?"

"Gee, this sounds like a really baffling mystery!" said Bess as they got out of the car.

"You can also see why we'll have to walk," said Nancy. "I'm afraid this cinder path is too rough and rutted to risk driving on."

"You said it," agreed George. "You'd wreck your springs."

The girls started out across the brief expanse of meadowland that adjoined the road and soon entered the woods. All three found themselves breathing deeply and enjoying the sylvan atmosphere as they walked along. The air was cool and filled with the songs of birds.

"This is really pleasant!" Bess said, sounding slightly surprised.

"See, there, what did I tell you?" asked George smugly. "If you'd try this sort of thing a little more often, you might actually get to *like* exercise!"

"Ugh!" Bess made a face at her cousin, and all three girls burst out laughing.

As they passed the rock quarry, Nancy

pointed out the few footprints that were visible where the ground was mushy, and also the tire tread marks.

"Do you figure the car or truck, whatever it was, came from Highway 19 and went back the same way?" George questioned Nancy.

"That's what it looks like," the teenage sleuth said and nodded, "because the tire tracks connect with the cinder path on that side of the quarry. If they'd joined the path on the side toward the house, I would have assumed the vehicle came from Possum Road. But hopefully, if we follow the path farther along, we may really stumble on a clue that will help us identify it."

About a quarter of a mile past the quarry, the three girls reached an old wooden bridge over Possum Creek.

Bess paused timidly. "Gee, that doesn't look very stable."

"You're right, it doesn't," Nancy agreed.

Ordinarily the creek was a small, bubbling stream, but the heavy rainfall over the weekend had turned it into a swollen torrent.

"Wow!" gulped Bess, venturing close enough to peer down at the muddy, rushing water.

After examining the bridge, Nancy saw that

the flood had weakened some of the bridge supports. "Maybe we'd better turn back," she decided. "Crossing it looks too risky."

But George strode boldly out onto the structure, saying, "Come on, don't be scaredy-cats! It's perfectly safe."

Even as she spoke, the bridge rattled ominously and gave way. With a scream, George plunged toward the swift waters below!

6

Windshield Warning

Nancy and Bess gasped in fear, but in the nick of time George managed to grab hold of a broken plank that was still part of the remaining bridge structure! With both arms stretched over her head and hanging on for dear life, George dangled perilously above the rain-swollen creek!

"Good girl!" shouted Nancy, finding her voice again. "I'll pull you up. Just don't let go!"

"Okay," George quavered in a strained voice. "But make it quick . . . *ple-e-e-ease!*"

Crouching down on all fours, Nancy scrambled out on what was left of the near side of the bridge, preparing to reach down and grab her friend by the wrists.

"Oh, Nancy, please be careful!" Bess begged tremulously.

"Don't worry, I think I can reach her! But if I can't get enough purchase, Bess, you may have to grab my ankles and haul back!"

Luckily, a fisherman who had seen the accident from the bank of the creek was already running toward them to lend a hand. "Hold tight, Miss!" he cried. "We'll soon have you up and safe!"

He scrambled out to the edge of the broken bridge alongside Nancy, and together they soon hauled George to safety.

"Oh, wow!" George panted as she sagged in a comical-looking heap. "What a scare I had, when the bridge gave way right under my feet!"

"A warning sign should have been put up first thing this morning," the fisherman declared indignantly. "I noticed when I first came here how rickety that thing looked. It was the storm that did it. Some of the bridge piles were already rotten, I guess, and the force of the flood water must've cracked 'em!"

"And I guess I was an idiot to venture out on the bridge when it was in such condition," George mumbled contritely, brushing herself off. "Anyhow, thanks ever so much to both of you for rescuing me!"

"Aw, don't mention it, young lady." The

fisherman grinned reassuringly, seeing her rueful expression. "Just be thankful your friend and I were around to help. If someone had tried to cross that bridge alone, it might've been a different story."

Smiling, Nancy added her own thanks for his help. The fisherman shook hands with all three girls and returned to his flycasting, after vowing to notify the police and the county road department that a warning sign should be posted before dark.

Nancy reflected privately that the authorities were probably not even aware that the bridge had been so near collapse. At any rate, Detective Hoyt didn't seem to know about it when he had discussed with Nancy the route taken by the mysterious, all-terrain vehicle.

Only one thing was certain, Nancy thought—no car of any kind could possibly have been driven across the bridge during the early morning hours of darkness. She definitely remembered that the storm had ended long before midnight, so by that time the damage to the bridge structure had already been done.

As the girls retraced their steps toward Possum Road, Nancy pondered what this discovery might tell her about Clare Grant's mysterious disappearance. For one thing, if no car could have crossed the bridge, this meant that the mystery vehicle must have come not from the direction of Highway 19 but from Possum Road, and must have left the woods by the same route.

When she pointed this out to her two chums, Bess looked puzzled. "But what about those tire tread marks, Nancy?" she asked. "You said yourself that they approached the quarry from the Highway 19 side."

"That's right, Bess. And they returned from the quarry to the cinder path on the same side. But, don't you see? If the driver had really come and gone that way, he and his vehicle would have ended up in Possum Creek."

"Wow! I see what you mean—and we know the bridge didn't break down until George tried to cross it just now."

"Exactly." Nancy nodded. "Therefore we know that the driver was deliberately trying to fool us—or to fool whomever went into the woods to look for Clare Grant."

"And what do you deduce from that, Nancy?" George queried.

The girl detective was silent for a moment before replying. "I'd say it could be very important," she mused. "It may mean that Clare Grant and her kidnappers—if she *was* kidnapped—may still be somewhere right in the vicinity of River Heights!"

Bess's eyes widened in surprise. "You mean

she may be hiding out somewhere?"

Nancy chuckled and shrugged. "To tell the truth, I don't know what I do mean—yet. Right now I can't even guess how or why Clare Grant disappeared. But at least we know a little more now than we did when we started out."

Trekking along the rutted cinder path, the trio passed the quarry and, minutes later, reached the fringe of the woods where the stand of trees thinned out. As they crossed the little stretch of meadow toward Possum Road, George pointed to the sleek blue sports car standing at the curb.

"Look, Nancy! Someone's stuck something under your windshield wiper!"

It looked like a folded piece of paper. Nancy hurried ahead to see what it was, wondering who could have left her a message. Plucking the paper out from under the wiper blade, she unfolded it, and her pretty face promptly took on a slightly troubled frown.

"Anything wrong?" asked George.

By way of reply, Nancy handed the paper to her and Bess. It bore two sets of initials: C.G. and N.D. A heavy, slanting line had been drawn through each.

"I don't get it," George muttered. "No, wait a minute! . . . Does the C.G. stand for 'Clare Grant'?"

"Of course!" Bess cut in excitedly. "And the N.D. must stand for 'Nancy Drew'!"

"But what about those lines through each set of initials?" George queried uneasily.

Nancy shrugged. "I suppose it could mean that Clare Grant's already been done away with, and I could be the next one to—disappear. At least that could be what whoever left this *wants* us to think."

"Oh, gee!" Bess Marvin's plump rosy cheeks paled slightly. "Nancy, are you sure you want to go on with this case? Maybe you should let the police find Clare Grant!"

Nancy's smile remained calm, though inwardly she felt her heart beating a bit faster than before. "You're forgetting, Bess, that it was the police who called me in in the first place."

"But they probably didn't realize then it might put you in danger!"

"Even so, I don't think I'll let myself be scared off just yet. Come on, let's go back to town before we melt."

"I second the motion!" said George.

Climbing into the car, Nancy turned on the air conditioner as the girls started back to River Heights.

"Didn't you say that's the house where Clare Grant was staying?" Bess inquired a few moments later as they passed the Fyfes' chateau.

"Yes," Nancy replied and saw that a red-and-white van was now parked in the driveway. It bore the name and insignia of the local television station, and below that in bold letters was the label: VIDEO NEWS.

"Looks like your latest mystery case is about to become a news item, Nancy," George remarked.

"So I see." Nancy was not quite sure whether to welcome or regret this development. It was too early to tell yet whether this might in any way hamper her investigation—or possibly, by encouraging people to come forward with information, even aid her in unraveling the mystery.

Her thoughts were suddenly interrupted as the car began to thump and wobble. The steering wheel had begun to shimmy violently in Nancy's hands. She gripped it firmly to keep the car on the road.

Bess gave a little cry of fright as the thumping and wobbling continued. "What's happening?"

"Don't know yet," Nancy said tersely. "Something seems to be wrong with the car."

"Oh, no-o-o!" Bess whimpered. "Maybe whoever stuck that note under the windshield tampered with the car while we were in the woods! Stop, Nancy, or it may blow up!"

7

A Sneaky Trick

"Bess, calm down! We'll be all right," George said, who was sitting in back. She reached forward and patted her cousin soothingly on the shoulder.

Nancy, meanwhile, was already applying the brakes. After bringing the car to a gradual stop as gently as possible, she got out to see what was wrong. The left front wheel seemed okay, but the right one was a different story.

"This tire is almost flat," she announced with a wry grin at her two friends. By this time, both had climbed out of the car.

"Shall we try to change it?" George inquired.

"No, I think that there's enough air left so that if I drive slowly, it won't hurt the wheel. It seems to me we passed a gas station on the way

58

out here. It's just a little way ahead, if I remember rightly, somewhere on the edge of town."

The trio got back into the car, and Nancy started up cautiously. Bess beamed a weak smile at her companions. "Sorry I threw such a wing-ding, but all that shaking and wobbling—well, I guess it sort of panicked me, especially after that scary note we found on the windshield!"

Nancy chuckled sympathetically. "Don't worry, I know just what you mean, Bess. To tell the truth, it kind of scared me, too."

Luckily, they soon reached the service station, and Nancy turned into it.

"Help you, Miss?" the grease-stained, cheerful-looking attendant asked Nancy as she got out of the car.

"I hope so," Nancy replied with a rueful smile. "As you see, I've got tire trouble."

The other two girls also climbed out as the attendant wheeled a tire jack up to the front end of the car. Before hoisting the right wheel, he bent down to pry off the hub cap and unscrew the lug nuts.

"Oh, oh!" he exclaimed suddenly. "This is probably what caused your trouble. Look here." He pointed to the tire valve.

Nancy gasped in chagrin and annoyance as

she saw the protruding end of a broken match-stick. The stick had been jammed in tightly in such a way as to hold the valve open and let the air slowly escape from the tire.

"Looks like somebody pulled a mean trick on you, Miss," said the attendant. "Too bad."

"Well, can you put some air in it, please . . ." Nancy broke off, then said decisively, "No, wait. I think you'd better put on my spare. I may have damaged this tire by driving on it while it was so low."

"Good idea," the man said and nodded. "And if you want to leave this one with me, I'll check it over—and also install a new valve stem assembly if this one's ruined. You can pick it up at your leisure."

"That'll be fine. I'm in kind of a hurry," Nancy said, glancing at her watch. She realized she would have to get home and dress quickly for her dinner date if she wanted to be ready when Ned came to pick her up.

The three girls were soon on their way with the spare wheel mounted in place of the flat. There was not enough time to play the mysterious video cassette for her two friends, so Nancy dropped Bess and George at their own homes and minutes later pulled into the drive of the Drew house.

After a word with Hannah about her father's

dinner, Nancy scampered upstairs to shower and change for her date with Ned. He had just arrived and was standing at the foot of the stairs, looking up at her admiringly as she came down in a new white cotton summer dress, with her red-gold hair gleaming from its last-minute brushing.

"I knew I forgot something!" he exclaimed.

"What did you forget?"

"My camera!"

Nancy giggled as he reached up to take her hands.

"I thought we might try Chan's tonight, Nancy," he went on as they started out the door. "But if Chinese food doesn't tempt you, we'll go wherever you like."

"No, that sounds wonderful, Ned." Nancy smiled as he helped her into his car. "I haven't had any moo goo gai pan in a long while, and I love it."

"Great. Then Chan's it is. We're on our way!"

It was close to ten-thirty that night when Nancy arrived back home. Over a delicious dinner and pots of Chinese tea, Ned had told her about his job interview that afternoon, and then they had discussed the latest developments in the Clare Grant disappearance.

When Nancy stepped in the front door after

bidding Ned good night, she was delighted to see Carson Drew sitting in the living room.

"Dad, I'm so glad you're still up. Have you got a moment to talk?" Nancy asked, sinking down on the comfortable sofa across from Carson Drew's chair and kicking off her shoes.

"Of course," her father answered. "Hannah mentioned that you went to dinner with Ned. Did you have a good time?"

"Oh, great! We went to Chan's and ate so much we had to roll ourselves out of there."

They both chuckled and went on chatting a few moments longer before Carson Drew said, "Well now, did you want to discuss something?"

Nancy nodded and began by bringing him up to date on the Clare Grant case. But she realized uncomfortably that she was just putting off what she had to say next. "Another thing, Dad . . . I know how this must sound, but—well, for some reason I just don't like Dallas Curry. On my way to lunch today, I actually worried that I might show how I felt about his stealing other people's ideas."

Carson Drew's expression was grave, and his eyebrows puckered in a faint look of concern.

"Does that upset you, Dad?"

"I must confess it does a bit, dear." He sighed thoughtfully. "Your feeling could well be based on some deep-down instinctive reaction, or let's just say feminine intuition in which case, it may mean my client is indeed guilty."

Carson Drew sat brooding in silence for a while. Then suddenly he slapped his hand on the arm of his chair and smiled at Nancy. "No matter, Dallas Curry is my client, and it's up to me to do all I can to prove he's innocent."

Nancy got up and rushed to hug him. "I'm glad of that. Because I just don't understand why I feel as I do. As I told you, all this was going through my mind as I drove to lunch . . . in other words, I was forming an opinion before I'd even heard all the facts in the case—which is crazy!"

Carson Drew stood up and kissed his daughter. "Crazy or not, no more worrying tonight," he said as he patted her back. "The day's over, and I propose to get a good sleep. I advise you to do the same."

"My sentiments precisely, Dad," she chuckled.

Next morning, Nancy breakfasted alone. Carson Drew had already left for the office, and Hannah was downstairs in the laundry room. So Nancy sat eating her poached egg and sipping her orange juice while she watched television. Clare Grant's disappearance was being given a big play on the local morning newscast.

The anchor person had just finished speaking of it when there was a knock on the screen door in the kitchen. "Anybody home?"

"Bess! You're just in time to join me for breakfast," Nancy said, hurrying to unhook the door.

Bess breezed into the house. "Oh, I've already eaten. But I'm thirsty enough to drink some of that orange juice. I guess that won't interfere with my diet, will it?"

Nancy grinned. "No danger!" She pulled out a chair and set a clean glass and napkin in front of Bess, then gestured toward the pitcher of cold juice. "Help yourself."

"Well, what's on the program today?" Bess inquired after her second swallow. "Can I help you on your latest mystery case, or would you like to go window shopping?"

"Actually I planned to report to Pamela Kane today about what we found out from our hike in the woods," Nancy replied. "Oh, oh—that reminds me. I meant to call Chief McGinnis this morning. Excuse me a minute, Bess."

Nancy was still uncertain in her own mind whether Clare Grant had disappeared from the Fyfes' house of her own free will, or whether she had been kidnapped by force. But there might be a way to check out one of those possibilities.

She dialed police headquarters and Chief McGinnis's voice soon came on the line. "Morning, Nancy. What can I do for you?"

"Chief, would it be possible to find out from all the taxicab companies around here if any of their drivers picked up a woman, either on Possum Road or somewhere on the outskirts of River Heights, during the early hours of Monday morning?"

"Sure, no problem. You're thinking of Clare Grant, eh?"

"Right. Whatever happened to her, I'm now convinced she left or was taken away via Possum Road, and not through the woods to Highway 19." Nancy told how the bridge over Possum Creek had been too weakened by the storm to have supported any car.

"Good work, Nancy," the police chief congratulated her. "I'll pass that information on to Detective Hoyt and let you know as soon as I learn anything from the cab companies."

Nancy and Bess quickly cleared the table and washed and dried the few dishes. Then after Nancy called down to tell Hannah Gruen that she was leaving, the two girls got into Nancy's car and started off toward Possum Road. As they reached the gas station where she had left the flat tire to be repaired, Nancy turned in.

"We may as well pick up that wheel and tire if they are ready."

They were. As she was paying the cheerful young attendant, a sudden idea passed through Nancy's mind. "Do you know anyone around here who has an off-the-road vehicle?" she asked.

The young man pondered a moment. "No, I can't think of anyone offhand—at least not any of our customers." Then he glanced hesitantly at the titian-blonde teenager. "Say, aren't you Nancy Drew, the detective?"

Nancy smiled and nodded.

"I thought I recognized you!" he said. "Hey, you wouldn't be working on the Clare Grant disappearance, would you? I just heard about that on TV this morning."

"Yes, I am. Did she ever come into the station here?" Nancy asked.

"Oh sure, quite a few times. Is that why you were asking about an off-the-road vehicle? I mean, does that have anything to do with her disappearance?"

Nancy hesitated, then decided to reveal a clue. She told the attendant about the tire tracks near the quarry in the woods, which apparently were made the same night that the actress vanished.

The attendant looked startled. "That could have been my service-station truck!"

66

8

Muddy Evidence

Nancy was startled by the station attendant's reply. "How do you know that?" she asked.

The man grinned and shrugged. "Well, I guess you might say I'm doing a little detective work myself, or at least putting two and two together." He pointed to the service truck, a small four-wheel-drive pickup. "When I closed the station on Saturday evening, I left it parked right there—under the station canopy. But I'd washed it before I left, so it was all nice and clean. Yet when I came back to open the station yesterday morning, it was all splashed with mud."

"How odd," said Nancy. The pickup was still dirty, its wheels and lower surfaces caked with grayish-tan streaks where the mud had dried and hardened; evidently the station attendant had not yet given the vehicle another washing. "Was it locked?"

"Yep, I'm always pretty careful about locking. 'Course that's no problem for an expert car thief. He can get the door open and hot-wire the ignition with no trouble at all."

As they talked, Nancy had begun walking toward the small truck. She wanted to examine its wide, deep-treaded tires. Seeing the direction of her interest, the attendant went on, "It's been driven pretty hard, all right. You can see how the tire treads are all plugged up with mud."

Nancy nodded thoughtfully. "Yes, I can see." What was more, she could see at a glance that the tread pattern matched that of the tracks in the woods, leading from the cinder path to the quarry and back. "Could any friends or—well, maybe teenage boys have done it for a prank?"

The attendant frowned and shook his head. "I doubt it . . . . Oh well, it's possible, I guess, but I sure can't think of anyone offhand who'd borrow the truck without asking me."

"Where do you keep the keys?"

"On a keyring in my pocket." He pulled a bunch of keys out to show her. "And there's an extra key hanging on a rack just inside the front door . . . but, of course, the station itself was locked up, too."

Seeing Nancy's expression, the attendant exclaimed keenly, "Did I guess right? You think it was my truck that made those tracks in the woods?"

"It certainly fills the bill."

Bess Marvin had been listening to the conversation between Nancy Drew and the station attendant. As the two girls drove away, she said, "Gee, it looks like you've just found another clue, Nancy! What do you make of all that?"

"I'm not sure myself yet, Bess—but it certainly seems to confirm my hunch that the vehicle came from Possum Road and not from Highway 19."

"But where on earth could the truck have taken Clare Grant?"

Nancy chuckled wryly. "If I knew the answer to that, Bess, I'd probably be close to solving the whole mystery!"

As they pulled up in front of the Fyfes' house a few minutes later, they saw a little red station wagon also parked in the drive.

"Does that belong to the people who live here?" Bess asked.

Nancy thought not, since the station wagon

69

looked neither very new nor well cared for. "I rather imagine Pamela Kane must have a visitor," she replied.

Her guess proved correct. When the housekeeper, Mrs. Barrow, answered the door, she said, "A reporter is interviewing Miss Kane. But she saw you out the window as you arrived and asked me to bring you right in."

The reporter turned out to be a sharp-featured young woman about twenty or twenty-one, with straight, glossy black hair and bangs fringing her forehead.

"This is Marcy Keech," Pamela introduced her to the new arrivals. "She wants to do a piece about Clare Grant's disappearance for *Limelight*."

"Oh, yes." Nancy had often seen the publication on sale at the supermarket. It was a weekly tabloid mainly devoted to gossip about show-business personalities. "You're one of their staff writers?"

"Not exactly." Marcy Keech seemed irritated at the question. "I'm a journalism student, actually, so I'm just working freelance for the summer. But the editor's very impressed with my talent, that's why he particularly wanted me to handle this assignment. Once I solve this case—which shouldn't be too hard—and scoop the rest of the press, he's as good as promised I can name my own salary."

Bess Marvin opened her baby-blue eyes suspiciously wide. "Gee, that sounds exciting, Miss Keech! Have you already figured out what happened to Clare Grant?"

"She got snatched, that's what happened!" snapped Marcy Keech. "It was obviously a professional job—either by racketeers connected with the mob, or else by independent hoods, maybe with show-biz connections."

"Oh! Just like in the movies!" Bess murmured more breathlessly than ever.

The reporter's only response was a tilted eyebrow and a supercilious sneer.

Nancy repressed a smile, sensing that Bess was only having a little fun at the other girl's expense. Aloud she said politely, "You may be right, Miss Keech."

"Of course I'm right! What other explanation is there?"

The teenager shrugged, refusing to be drawn into an argument. "I'm afraid I have no definite theory yet . . . except that the answer may lie closer to River Heights than we thought at first."

"What's that supposed to mean?" Marcy Keech challenged.

71

Nancy hesitated, not liking to make statements to the press while she was still investigating a case. But Pamela Kane was looking at her anxiously, as if eager for news, so Nancy went ahead and spoke. "You remember when we examined those tire tracks at the quarry yesterday, we assumed that the car came from the direction of Highway 19 and went back the same way?"

Pamela nodded, her brown eyes peering intently at Nancy through their pearl-rimmed pixie glasses. "Yes, what about it?"

"Apparently we were wrong."

"How do you know?"

"Yesterday afternoon, Bess and I and another girl decided to check out that cinder path in the woods between the quarry and Highway 19. We were hoping we might find some clues. But that path goes over an old wooden bridge that was damaged by the weekend storm—in fact, it was so weak it collapsed when one of us tried to walk over it. So there's no way any car could have driven over it in those early hours of darkness on Monday morning."

Pamela Kane looked bewildered. "But I . . . I don't understand. If the car didn't come from Highway 19, what are you implying?"

"That it came from Possum Road," Nancy replied patiently. "I'm almost certain, in fact, that it was a small, four-wheel-drive pickup truck from that gas station on the way into town. There's clear evidence that the truck was taken from the station and driven over muddy terrain sometime during the weekend. That's why I say the answer to the mystery may lie closer to River Heights than we thought."

Pamela was silent a moment while she digested this news. Then she burst out in a shocked, upset voice, "No, that doesn't make sense! Why would the kidnapper bring her back here where the police are looking for her and there's much more chance of being caught?"

"By now Clare Grant's picture has been published in newspapers and shown on TV, and police all over the country are looking for her," Nancy pointed out. "I doubt if the locale makes all that much difference."

Nancy went on to mention the famous mystery story, *The Purloined Letter*, in which the author, Edgar Allan Poe, pointed out the advantage of hiding something in plain sight in the most obvious place, where searchers might least think of looking for it.

But Pamela Kane stubbornly shook her head. Because of her own apparent fear for her friend's safety, she seemed to feel that Nancy was too lightly overlooking the danger Clare might be in. "No, I don't care what you say about the bridge," she exclaimed in a tearful voice, "you'll never convince me that Clare's safe and sound here in River Heights! I told you what she said on the phone about being threatened—she *knew* she was in danger, and she was frightened!"

Pamela paused with a gulp and reached for her hanky. She dabbed her eyes, then blew her nose and shook her head again. "Why would anyone around here want to kidnap a Broadway actress? No, I just don't believe it!"

"Neither do I," Marcy Keech cut in scornfully. "If you ask me, Miss Drew's so used to her small-town, amateurish mystery-dabbling that she doesn't realize more serious crimes get committed every day."

Nancy shrugged and kept her temper in check, refusing to let the journalism student's unfair criticism bother her.

"The fact that the bridge is unsafe just means that someone deliberately tried to mislead us," she said evenly. "You can draw any conclusion you like from that, I suppose. But the simplest one certainly seems to be that Clare Grant *wasn't* taken away from River Heights."

Marcy Keech responded with a contemptuous sniff. "That's all *you* know," she sneered. "Maybe you'd better take a look at what I found under Clare's bedroom window. Then tell us if you still don't think she was forcibly abducted by skilled professional crooks!"

As she spoke, Marcy Keech rose from her chair and stepped over to the small table where she had placed her hat and shoulder bag. Reaching into her bag, she pulled out a metal can. "If you didn't want to use a weapon that might cause serious injury, what would be the quickest way to render a kidnap victim helpless?" she asked.

With a triumphant smirk, by way of an answer to her own question, she displayed the label on the metal container to Nancy.

Her find was a spray can of ether!

9

Smear Tactic

Nancy's eyes widened in surprise as she stood up for a closer look at the spray can that Marcy Keech was holding out toward her. Bess and Pamela Kane also rose and gathered around the other two, as the young detective considered this unexpected new item of evidence.

"Ether!" Nancy murmured. She had seen the same sort of product before at gas stations and auto-supply stores. It was intended to help stalled motorists start their cars at cold temperatures by spraying the vapor directly into their carburetors.

But ether was also an anesthetic that could, indeed, render a person unconscious!

Well, well! Things were beginning to look

more serious, Nancy reflected. This could certainly mean that Clare Grant had been kidnapped!

"You see, Nancy?" Pamela burst out in a voice that was almost a wail. "Maybe now you can understand why I'm so upset! ... Oh, I knew it right from the first! Something terrible's happened to Clare!"

"Nonsense," Bess said, trying to take a calmer, more sensible view. "This can by itself doesn't prove anything."

Nancy, for her part, was busy thinking. How could she and Detective Hoyt have missed seeing so obvious a clue yesterday morning? They had taken time to look in the shrubbery and tall grass under Clare's window before starting off toward the woods. She was almost positive the can hadn't been there then.

"What are you going to do with it?" Nancy asked the sharp-nosed reporter evenly.

"What am I going to do with it?" Marcy echoed with a mocking sneer. "Turn it over to the police, that's what!"

"Then wouldn't it have been wiser not to touch it and spoil any fingerprints that were on it?" Nancy suggested in a quiet voice.

Bess turned a smiling face to the journalism student. "That does make sense, doesn't it?"

Marcy Keech flushed a deep, angry red. Then she turned abruptly and flounced off toward the nearest chair, the one Bess had been sitting in. As she sat down with a thump, there was a rustle of paper.

A frown of suspicion spread over her face. Springing up, she turned to look at the chair seat. There, nestled in its wrapper, lay a gooey piece of chocolate candy bar—now squashed flat! With an outraged gasp, she craned her neck around and tugged at the skirt of her dress in order to examine the results of her mishap. The material was visibly stained with chocolate.

Furiously she turned toward Bess. "Really! I believe you did that on purpose!" she interrupted the blonde girl's apologies.

"Oh, no!" Bess exclaimed in sympathetic dismay. "I'm so sorry. You see, I was looking through my purse for a piece of tissue, and then when you showed us the spray can, I jumped up to see it, and the candy must have fallen out of my purse onto the chair."

She broke off helplessly as Marcy interrupted. "May I use your powder room?" she asked Pamela Kane curtly and rushed out of the living room.

Bess quickly removed the offending chocolate bar from the chair and was *very* relieved that none had stuck to the upholstery. She muttered to Nancy, "I *would* have felt bad if it had stained the chair." Nancy smiled quietly in agreement. Then, after assuring Pamela that she would continue her investigation and do everything possible to find Clare Grant, the teenage sleuth got up to leave with Bess.

"Oh, I do hope you find her soon!" Pamela fretted anxiously. "I'm so afraid she's fallen into the hands of criminals, just like Marcy Keech says. That's what I told the police right from the first!"

"Believe me, they're doing all they can," Nancy said. "In the meantime, it would help if you'd try and remember anything at all that Clare said on the phone that might clue us in as to whom or what she was afraid of."

"I'll try my best," Pamela promised.

Nancy was silent and thoughtful as she and Bess drove down the tree-lined road toward River Heights. Why, she wondered, was Pamela Kane so insistent that her friend had been kidnapped? Was it possible that she knew something more about the mystery than she was willing to let on? Perhaps it would be a good idea to learn more about Clare Grant's visitor from California!

As they entered the streets of town, Bess said,

"Nancy, I'm meeting George at Bonnington's department store. Why don't you come along, and we'll all shop and have lunch there?"

"I wish I could, Bess, but I think I'd better try to make some progress on the case I'm working on with Dad."

"Well, okay. I'll call you tomorrow then."

After letting Bess out in the downtown section of River Heights, Nancy drove home. As soon as she had parked and hurried into the house, she went to the hall telephone and dialed her father's office. His secretary put her through immediately.

"Dad, I'm sorry to bother you, but I need a little help."

"You name it, honey," Carson Drew replied.

"It's about the Clare Grant case. I have a funny feeling that her friend, Pamela Kane, may know more than she's telling. Could you have your regular firm of private investigators do a little digging into her background? I mean very discreetly, of course, so she won't find out and get any more upset than she already is."

"Certainly, I can have the agency run a check on her. Just a moment while I get my pen. You say her name is Pamela Kane, eh? What can you tell me about her?"

"Not much, I'm afraid. She flew in yesterday

morning from Los Angeles where she lives. I gather she and Clare Grant became friendly out there while Clare was working in the movies, and they shared an apartment for a while."

"Do you know her address?"

"Gee, no, I don't," Nancy replied. "In fact, I don't even know what airline she flew East on."

"Well, no matter. That shouldn't be too hard to find out. But a description of Pamela Kane might help."

"Oh, of course. She's about as tall as I am, in her twenties, with long blonde hair . . . and she wears pearl-rimmed pixie glasses. She's an actress, too—or a would-be actress, anyhow."

"Good. Do you remember what she was wearing yesterday when you first saw her?"

"Yes, a blue-and-white patterned shirtwaist dress with short sleeves and a belt. Her luggage was sitting in the front hall when I arrived, with her jacket and hat on top of it, so I can describe those, too. Her suitcase was light blue, and she had a navy blue jacket and white hat."

"Excellent detail," Mr. Drew commented. "That should give the agency operatives plenty to go on. They'll probably start at the airport and backtrack from there."

"Thanks a lot, Dad," Nancy said.

"Care to come down here for lunch with me?"

"Oh, I'd love to! But I thought I'd just have a quick bite here and go to New York this afternoon. I want to visit those ad agencies Dallas Curry mentioned and see if I can pick up any useful information."

"I see. Well, be careful, dear. Just remember, Manhattan's not the safest place in the world these days."

"I'll be careful, Dad," Nancy promised and signed off with a kiss.

After a check of shuttle flight schedules and a hasty lunch with Hannah, she set off for the airport in her sleek blue sports car. Two hours later, Nancy was walking down Madison Avenue in the very heart of the midtown skyscraper district. Her first stop was to be the Darby & Wallace advertising agency. This was the one that had produced the original Statue of Liberty fashion ad.

As she went up in the elevator to their fourteenth-floor offices, Nancy was thinking about what questions she would ask.

In the firm's nicely furnished waiting room, she explained to the receptionist why she had come and asked to speak to the head of the agency. After a short wait in the nearest burgundy leather chair, she was told that he was too busy to see her without an appointment, but that the executive vice-president, Mr. Knapp, who dealt with the firm's legal affairs, would be glad to talk to her.

Knapp greeted her in friendly fashion when she was ushered into his office and invited her to sit down. "I've heard about you and your talent for solving mysteries, Miss Drew, and it's a pleasure to meet you. I'm not sure how much of a mystery there is about our unfortunate problem with Dallas Curry, but we're certainly willing to do whatever we can to clear it up."

He added that he had already phoned the two agency staffers who had been most closely concerned with the Statue of Liberty ad to join them in his office.

"Thank you," said Nancy. "If they can shed any light on how the duplication happened, I'll certainly appreciate it."

The firm's chief copywriter, Roscoe Leff, arrived first. He was a plump man in his thirties with thinning hair. Though stylishly dressed, he was in his shirtsleeves with his collar open at the neck and his tie loosened, which gave him a busy air, as if he could spare her only a few minutes from his crowded schedule.

"Can you tell me exactly how the ad was created, Mr. Leff?" Nancy asked.

"Sure, no problem. The account executive told us in a general way what the client was looking for, so the following afternoon about a half-dozen of us got together for a brainstorming session—you know, just firing ideas back and forth."

Roscoe Leff paused and shrugged. "As it turned out, I came up with the idea for this Statue of Liberty layout pretty fast, and everyone went for it right away. I had an artist rough it out, and our staff photographer shot it the very next day."

As he finished speaking, he glanced toward the door. "Here's the photographer now—Rick Hyatt. I imagine he can tell you anything more you want to know."

A lanky young man with bleached blond hair had just walked into the office. Nancy stared at him for a moment, too surprised to speak.

Rick Hyatt was the cameraman who had snapped her picture in River Heights the day before, and then fled in his yellow convertible!

10

A Frustrating Afternoon

"So you're a professional cameraman, Mr. Hyatt," Nancy challenged him with a slight edge to her voice. "Am I to assume those pictures you were taking yesterday were also for this agency?"

Both Mr. Knapp and Roscoe Leff looked startled at Nancy's remark. Knapp knit his brows in a puzzled frown. "You two know each other?" he queried, glancing from the girl detective to the lanky photographer, and back to Nancy.

"Let's just say we had a brief encounter yesterday," she replied. "He snapped my picture outside my father's office. Before that, he was at a restaurant where Dad and I lunched with Dallas Curry. My father, you see, is acting as Mr. Curry's legal counsel. Since Mr. Hyatt behaved quite furtively and drove off in a hurry when I spotted him, I rather imagine he must have been photographing all three of us at the restaurant."

"What's this all about, Hyatt?" Mr. Knapp demanded sharply.

The photographer shuffled his feet and scowled down at the carpet. "What Miss Drew says is true enough—I *was* photographing them. But I had Monday off, remember, a three-day weekend. So I was doing it on my own time."

"Why?"

The tall, blond young man hesitated sullenly, then shrugged. "As soon as Curry's case comes to trial, he'll be big news."

"That's no reason to hound the man," Knapp retorted with a frown of disapproval. "He may or may not be guilty of copying other people's work. I'm willing to suspend judgment on that. If he *is* guilty, he may have acted under some emotional strain that we know nothing about. The fact remains that Dallas Curry is still one of America's greatest photographers—nothing can alter that!"

Roscoe Leff nodded, though he seemed less concerned than the agency vice-president about Rick Hyatt's surreptitious picture-snapping. "He's right, Rick. Dallas Curry made his reputation the hard way, and it's not up to us to tear it down. If he's guilty of stealing ideas or layouts, the court will punish him—that's out of our hands now."

"Curry's reputation has been blown way out of proportion!" Hyatt sneered. "He lucked out with a few sensational news shots, and everyone started calling him an artist with a camera. But the truth is, he's just a photographic hack—and now that he's run out of ideas, he's proved it by swiping those magazine layouts!"

At first, Rick Hyatt's face had reddened with embarrassment when Nancy recognized him. She was sure she detected a note of jealousy in his snide remarks about Dallas Curry.

"You can tell your father and Curry, too, that I intend to photograph every aspect of this legal mess he's got himself into," Hyatt said to Nancy. "As a matter of fact, I've already got an order from the *National Scanner* for a complete picture story on his case when it comes to trial."

The *National Scanner,* as Nancy well knew, was a photo magazine more devoted to covering scandals than to telling the truth.

"Then it's obvious I'll be wasting my time if I expect any impartial information from you, Mr.

Hyatt," she said coolly. After thanking the other two for their help, she rose and walked out of the office.

As she closed the door behind her, she could hear Knapp begin taking the young photographer harshly to task, both for his discourteous attitude toward Nancy and for his moonlighting assignment.

Nancy went next to the Stratton Agency, which was located only two blocks away. This was the advertising firm that had created the original Knights of the Round Table ad for a furniture manufacturer.

After her introduction to an account executive named Ted Yates, she was directed to John Stratton, the president of the agency. He was perfectly willing to talk to her and received her in his office after only a short wait. "I see no reason to be unpleasant about this, Miss Drew," he told the teenage sleuth, "but the matter is out of our hands now. As you may have heard, we've filed a charge of ethical misconduct against the firm that handled Curry's layout for pirating our ad."

"You're convinced that it *was* a case of pirating?" Nancy inquired politely.

"Absolutely! No question about it," Mr. Stratton firmly stated.

"But Mr. Curry would have to have seen your

ad somehow in order to copy it," Nancy pointed out. "How do you think he got hold of it before it was published?"

"We already know the answer to that question," Mr. Stratton replied. "Our agency suffered a break-in just about that time. Our security man discovered that a door lock had been jimmied the morning after it happened. And later, our production department discovered that a copy of the layout was missing."

"So once Dallas Curry's version of the same layout was published, you decided he was the thief?"

Stratton looked slightly uncomfortable at Nancy's blunt use of the word "thief," but he threw up his hands in a helpless, shrugging gesture. "Well, more likely he hired someone to commit the actual break-in, I suppose. It boils down to the same thing. What else are we to think?"

"But why on earth would a famous photographer of Dallas Curry's reputation do such a thing?" Nancy argued.

"Your guess is as good as mine, Miss Drew. Perhaps the Advertising Council will come up with an answer when it finishes investigating the ethical misconduct charge we've filed."

Marc Joplin, Incorporated—the last of the

three agencies involved in the strange series of duplicated ad layouts—was located on East 42nd Street within sight of Grand Central Station. This was the firm that was suing Dallas Curry for copying its cosmetic flower-face ad.

A youthful, husky-looking man with curly chestnut hair came out to the waiting room to speak to Nancy. He introduced himself as Oliver Snell, the firm's art director. His manner was coldly polite.

"I've no wish to be rude, Miss Drew," he said, "but we know that your father is Dallas Curry's attorney. So I hardly think it would be wise to discuss our lawsuit with you."

"I see." Nancy was silent a moment, choosing her next words with care. "Can you at least tell me the background circumstances of your client's ad and who created it?"

"*I* did . . . at least the idea was mine, and I sketched out the layout before it was photographed. In fact, I imagine I'll be the principal witness at Curry's trial—which is why the receptionist called me when you told her why you were here. But I think that will also explain," Snell ended, "why I had better not talk to you any further."

"I quite understand," Nancy said and nodded as they exchanged a brief parting handclasp.

"Sorry I bothered you, Mr. Snell, and thank you for your time."

Feeling frustrated and somewhat depressed, she flew back to River Heights, arriving home just in time to join Carson Drew and Hannah Gruen at the dinner table.

"Well, how did you do in New York, dear?" her father inquired as she drew up a chair and spread her napkin on her lap.

Nancy sighed. "Not too well, I'm afraid, Dad." She filled him in on her visits to the three advertising agencies and added, "The trouble is I can't even think of any explanation myself, other than out-and-out copying ... which makes it pretty hard to think of any useful questions to ask."

Mr. Drew nodded grimly. "Yes, I know exactly what you mean. I find myself up against the same problem."

"You know, Dad," Nancy went on thoughtfully as she ladled out some of Hannah's delicious roast-beef gravy over her mashed potatoes, "I believe I'll tell Dallas Curry personally about my experiences today at those agencies. It might just start some fresh train of thought in his mind that would help him come up with a useful new lead."

"Good idea. It certainly can't do any harm."

As soon as dinner was over, Nancy dialed the famed photographer's home number. When he answered, she told him about her trip to Manhattan and asked if she might drop over that evening to discuss the outcome.

"By all means!" Curry responded and gave her precise directions for finding his house.

Nancy was about to leave a few minutes later when the doorbell rang. Bess Marvin and George Fayne were standing outside under the porch light. She could see from a mere glance at their faces that both were upset, especially Bess.

"Did you hear the news tonight on TV?" her blonde friend blurted indignantly before she had even stepped inside.

"No, why?" said Nancy. "Is something wrong?"

"You bet there is! You know that Marcy Keech creature we bumped into this morning when you went to see Pamela Kane?"

"Of course. What's she done now?"

"She's taking all the credit for finding the truck that made those tracks in the woods—that's what!"

11

Telephone Reports

Nancy felt mildly irritated by the young woman reporter's boastful fib. But compared to her frustrating trip to New York that afternoon, the whole thing seemed too unimportant to get upset about.

"Never mind, Bess," she said with a rueful smile. "When and if any of those TV news people go out to interview that gas-station attendant and photograph his service truck, I'm sure he'll put them right."

"Of course he will," Bess realized aloud, looking suddenly more cheerful. "I never thought of that!"

"I'd ask you two to sit down," Nancy explained as her two friends came into the living room, "but I was just about to take off."

"Where to?" George inquired breezily.

"To see Dad's client—that photographer, Dallas Curry. Want to come along?"

"Hey, yes! He should be an interesting guy to meet. . . . If you're sure he won't mind?"

"I'm sure. Just wait a second till I slip on a sweater and get my bag."

Dallas Curry's home was an imposing, modernistic house built of redwood and cement blocks. Nancy reached it by following a long, winding drive that led from the main road into the very heart of his sprawling, wooded estate.

A white-coated Japanese houseman opened the door to the girls' ring, but Curry himself came promptly to greet his guests and escort them into his comfortable, firelit living room. He seemed happy to have visitors and delighted that Nancy had brought along her two friends.

"The more the merrier!" he declared, his handsome, deeply tanned face creasing into a jovial smile. He insisted on having his houseman serve the girls refreshments. Nancy and George settled for iced tea while Bess—dimpling guiltily—accepted a marshmallow fudge sundae.

"Now then, tell us about your agency talks in New York, Nancy," said the host. "Did you turn up any clues?"

"Not really—at least nothing that gives me any definite leads to follow." She reported what had occurred at each of the three advertising agencies she had visited. Dallas Curry listened with keen interest.

When she was through, Nancy asked, "This Rick Hyatt—who's so eager to get a picture story on the lawsuit—do you know him?"

Curry shook his head. "Never met the chap so far as I know."

"He seemed awfully down on you."

The photographer shrugged. "He's entitled to his opinion."

"If you ask me, he sounds jealous," put in Bess with a spoonful of fudge sundae poised in midair.

"Could be," Dallas Curry agreed. "I suppose he feels big assignments come my way too easily. He doesn't realize how much hard work it took to make a name for myself in the first place."

With a crooked grin, Curry added, "Not that I'll have much reputation left if I lose this lawsuit!"

"One thing did strike me," Nancy mused aloud. "There was the definite break-in at the Stratton Agency—which they discovered the morning after it happened—and a copy of their Round Table layout was missing. But the other two firms don't even have any theory as to how you could have gotten hold of their layouts in order to copy them."

"That's not surprising, since I didn't."

"But in each case, the layouts are very much alike," Nancy pointed out. "I mean they *look* very much alike. Stealing an idea is one thing. But here the appearance is so similar that it almost seems as though you would have had to *see* the other layouts in order to copy them so closely."

"What are you suggesting?" said George with a puzzled expression. "Some form of ESP, like mental telepathy?"

Nancy smiled helplessly and shook her red-gold hair. "Somehow, to get to the bottom of this mystery, we're going to have to find out how two different people, who photograph an advertising layout, could have the *same mental image* of how they want it to look. After all, the similarity is in the *picture*, not in the wording or arrangement of the advertising copy."

"It sounds pretty weird when you put it like that," Curry commented ruefully. "It almost seems as though there'd either have to be an out-and-out theft of a sketch or layout beforehand, or else some kind of mental telepathy like George just mentioned."

"Did you yourself have a sketch of each layout to work from before you took the actual pictures?" Nancy inquired.

"No, that's one advantage of having a well-known name and reputation in this business. The agencies who hire me generally give me a free hand." Dallas Curry chuckled dryly. "Of course, they or their clients may not like what I come up with, but I get my fee just the same. After all, that's what they're paying me for—to be, shall we say, *creative*."

He gave the word a comical emphasis that made the girls laugh.

"Well, never mind—that's enough shop talk for one evening. How would you young ladies like to see and hear some music . . . and while we're at it, I'll give Nancy another little mystery to solve."

Curry rose from his chair, inserted a tape cassette into his video recorder, and proceeded to play the tape over his television set. It proved to be a series of colorful videos filmed and recorded by various rock bands. Nancy and her chums sat back to enjoy their performance.

"Are you a rock fan, Mr. Curry?" asked Bess, who by now had finished her sundae.

"Very much so." He chuckled again, this time more lightheartedly. "I guess some of my friends think I'm too old for such nonsense, but like it or not, I'm hooked. I think rock music is a genuine form of artistic expression."

The famed photographer explained that one of his early assignments for *Glance* magazine had been to photograph a popular rock group on concert tour. Hearing them perform had gradually turned him into an enthusiast. Later, he had photographed other groups and singers, and eventually had published a book of these pictures, which had become a worldwide best-seller.

"You said something about a mystery," put in George.

Dallas Curry nodded. "Right. The mystery is who sent me this tape cassette."

Nancy was startled by his words. "You mean it came by mail—anonymously?"

"Yes, and not just this one. I've received several during the past year, I guess. No names on the packages, no notes enclosed—nothing. I've never been able to find out who sent them."

"That's strange," Nancy murmured. "I got one, too. It just came yesterday—by special delivery."

It was Dallas Curry's turn to be surprised. "Same way mine came!" he said. "Then you've already been confronted with this particular mystery."

"Yes, though I must confess I haven't really made any attempt to solve it yet. But now that I know the same thing's happened to you, I certainly intend to try."

Curry laughed. "Well, no rush—I'm not complaining. Matter of fact, I've photographed all these groups. Whoever sent these videos must know just who my favorite bands are. I've played the tapes over and over again."

Curry's mention of the rock groups he had photographed led to amusing stories and anecdotes about other experiences during his career as a news, magazine, and advertising photographer. It was clear that he was putting himself out to entertain his guests. Nancy suspected that he had probably been feeling somewhat depressed over the pending lawsuit and the threat to his professional reputation, and that this evening's visit by her and her friends had provided a welcome diversion.

The talk ranged far and wide, with the girls contributing as much to the lively chatter as their host. Later, the houseman served a tasty snack to top off the evening, and by the time the three visitors drove away, it was past eleven o'clock.

"He's really fun to be around!" Bess exclaimed. "I like him."

"So do I," said George. "I think those charges of his stealing anyone else's ideas are a lot of hot air, don't you, Nancy? He seems too talented to stoop to such a thing!"

Nancy was a bit embarrassed and shamefaced to admit that her own opinion of Dallas Curry was less favorable. But she also admitted that her feelings about him were gradually, it seemed, becoming less negative than before.

The next morning, Nancy slept in later than usual. As she was eating breakfast, Chief McGinnis called from police headquarters. "We've got some feedback from the taxicab companies," he reported.

"Oh, yes," Nancy said eagerly. "Did any of the drivers remember a passenger who resembled Clare Grant?"

"No. You remember you asked about a woman being picked up either on Possum Road or somewhere on the outskirts of River Heights? The only one who comes close to that is a young woman who boarded a cab at the bus station around five-thirty in the morning and was driven from there to the airport. But, of course, the bus depot is eight or ten blocks from the edge of town, and her description didn't match Clare Grant's at all."

Nancy was disappointed, but said good-naturedly, "Well, thanks anyway, Chief. It seemed like a possibility worth following up, even if it didn't pay off."

"You bet. That's the way most crimes get solved, Nancy, as you well know—by patiently checking out all possibilities."

Only a few minutes after she had hung up, the telephone rang again. This time the caller was Carson Drew. "My private investigators have just phoned me a report on Pamela Kane, Nancy," he said.

"Gee, fast work, Dad! Did they have any trouble?"

"None at all. They located the airline she flew on and found out that her flight reservation had been made at a certain travel agency in Los Angeles. Apparently the travel agency gave them her address."

"Did your investigators check it out?"

"Yes. Remember, you told me that she and Clare Grant used to be roommates? Well, since Clare moved East, Pamela apparently has been sharing an apartment with two other young women. One of them's still in Los Angeles, but the other also recently came East. She's a dancer named Sylvia Salmo. She went to New York to try to get a job on Broadway."

"I see." Nancy digested this news in silence for a moment, then said, "Well, so at any rate

102

your investigators turned up nothing suspicious about Pamela?"

"No, apparently she's just what she claims to be—a friend of Clare Grant's who came here from California to visit her."

"Okay, Dad. Thanks for your help. See you at dinner." Putting down the phone, Nancy debated her next move. Perhaps it might be worthwhile to return to the scene of Clare's disappearance to see if any fresh clues had turned up.

After a word to Hannah, she backed her blue sports car out of the garage and started out toward Possum Road. A short while later, when she rang the bell at the Fyfes' house, Pamela Kane herself opened the door.

"Oh, Nancy! I'm so glad you're here," she exclaimed and led the way into the spacious living room. "I have something to show you!"

"What is it?"

"Well, I was searching through Clare's personal things, hoping that I might discover something that would give us a hint of what's happened to her, and I found this piece of paper with a phone number on it." Pamela picked up a slip of paper from a table and held it out with an eagerly hopeful expression.

Nancy glanced at the number. "Hmm, a 212

area code. That means it's a New York City number."

"Do you think it's important?"

"There's one way to find out. Mind if I use the phone?"

"Please do!" Pam gestured toward a white phone on a side table near an easy chair.

Nancy went over, picked up the handset, and dialed the number. There was only a single ring. Then her eyes widened in surprise as a man's voice answered: "Oliver Snell here."

12

The Elusive Clue

Oliver Snell! It took an instant for the name and the voice to register, then her pulse quickened. Quietly Nancy put down the receiver, a frown clouding her face.

What was Clare Grant's connection with the art director of the Marc Joplin advertising agency? True, the Statue of Liberty layout that Clare had posed for was one that Dallas Curry was accused of stealing, but that ad had nothing to do with Oliver Snell's firm.

Her thoughts were interrupted by Pamela Kane's voice. "Who was it, Nancy?" she repeated insistently. "Why did you hang up?"

"Because the man who answered is involved in another case I'm working on," Nancy said. "His name is Oliver Snell. He's employed by an ad agency in New York." Briefly she filled Pamela in on the lawsuit that had been filed against Dallas Curry for allegedly pirating three magazine ad layouts.

"But don't you want to question him about Clare and find out if he knows anything about her disappearance?" Pamela protested emotionally.

"Yes, indeed I do," said Nancy, "and I intend to—but not over the phone, and not until I've thought this thing through a bit more. It might also help to dig up a little more background information before I approach Mr. Snell again."

She explained that, when investigating mysteries, she usually found it better to question witnesses face to face, in order to observe their reactions and thus have more to go on in judging whether or not they were telling the truth.

"Also," Nancy added with a wry grin, "sometimes it's wiser not to tip one's hand in advance. If Oliver Snell doesn't know that his phone number was found among Clare Grant's effects, he won't be on his guard—and perhaps he'll talk a little more freely."

Pamela Kane nodded anxiously. "Yes, I see what you mean, and that does make sense, all right. But do, please, talk to him soon, Nancy! Somehow I have a feeling that this lead may be very important!"

"Don't worry," Nancy said, squeezing the blonde woman's hand reassuringly, "I promise I'll check it out thoroughly and find out if Snell had anything to do with Clare's disappearance. When I learn anything, I'll let you know as soon as possible, Pam."

Nancy left the Fyfes' house soon afterward, with an inward sigh of relief. She found Pamela's nervous, nagging manner anything but conducive to serious thinking about the mysteries she was trying to solve. Also, she was eager to pursue a fresh line of investigation that had occurred to her.

Instead of returning home, Nancy drove to Ashton University, which was located in a small community of the same name not far from River Heights. Last night, while puzzling over Dallas Curry's plight, she had remembered reading that the Ashton faculty included a well-known psychology professor, Dr. Hugh Jaffee, who was spending part of the summer conducting experiments with interested and willing students.

Jaffee had published a number of papers on some obscure quirks of the mind that seemed to defy scientific explanation. Because of this and his fame as a research psychologist, Nancy had decided to seek his opinion on the Curry case. Although the chance that he could shed any light on the mystery seemed slim, still she felt that no avenue of inquiry should be overlooked.

When she inquired at the university office, Nancy found that he was in and would be happy to see her. Following the clerk's instructions, she walked the short distance to the ivy-covered brick building that housed the psychology department.

There, a student in the entrance hallway directed her to a large room. Inside it, a dozen or more young men and women of college age, in casual summer dress, were sitting in individual, three-sided booths. They wore earphones, and their lips were moving as they read aloud from books.

Dr. Hugh Jaffee turned out to be a small, thin, gray-haired man with boundless energy and enthusiasm for his work. He was pacing up and down the room, obviously deep in thought and paying no attention to the babble as he jotted down notes from time to time on a memo pad.

It was a few moments before he noticed Nancy. Then his eyes lit up and he came striding over to greet her with a brisk handshake. "Ah, Miss Drew! How nice to meet you in person. I've read a great deal about this interesting talent you have for solving mysteries."

"I've read about you, too, Dr. Jaffee," Nancy replied with a smile. "That's why I came. I'm hoping you can help me solve a mystery."

"Indeed? Well, I'm a psychologist, not a detective, Miss Drew, but I'll be delighted to help you in any way I can." With a glance and a gesture toward the students in the booths, he went on, "Perhaps we'd better go to my private office, where we can hear ourselves think."

As they walked toward a doorway at the other end of the room, Nancy asked curiously, "What are they listening to?"

"A recording of a voice reading from a history textbook, though the subject doesn't really matter. The object of the experiment is to see how much—if anything—that's said over the earphones will be retained in the student's subconscious mind."

As he held open the door for Nancy to go through, Dr. Jaffee continued, "I might add, the tonal quality of the voice is soft and low. Anything strident would get their total attention . . . which, of course, would spoil the whole purpose of the experiment."

When they were seated comfortably in his private office, Nancy explained the trouble that Dallas Curry was in. "He's very worried, Dr. Jaffee, and swears he's innocent," she concluded. "Even if one doesn't believe him, there's no reason why he should do such a thing. His own work is too highly regarded and too much in demand for him to have to copy anyone else's. Can you think of any other explanation of what happened?"

The professor had listened with keen interest to Nancy's story. He proceeded to ask her several questions. Then he sat for a while with his head bowed in thought and his forefingers steepled under his chin.

"I'm not at all sure I can be of much help, Miss Drew," he commented at last. "I'm bound to say that, despite all you've told me, this sounds more like a leak in security somewhere along the line than any unusual process of thought transference."

"Then you believe Dallas Curry must be lying?"

Jaffee frowned and shook his head. "Not at all. But I do think he may have seen or been exposed to a glimpse of those rival layouts at some time or other and just doesn't remember it. Oh, there have been cases on record—well-known cases, in fact—of two or more people thinking along the same lines, each unaware of the other"—Dr. Jaffee waved his hand in the air—"like Darwin and Wallace, for instance, both coming up with the theory of evolution at the same time. But I doubt very much that that was what happened with Mr. Curry."

Nancy nodded, a little discouraged.

"Also, of course," the professor went on, "in the field of parapsychology—which is the study of extrasensory perception, such as mental telepathy and so on—researchers are trying to explain a number of odd 'coincidences' that keep turning up. But so far nothing definite has been proven. Let me think about this some more, Miss Drew, and I'll call you if I get any ideas."

Nancy thanked him, gave him her phone number, and left. On the drive home, she decided to relax and enjoy the sunny day and put both of her vexing mystery cases out of her mind. But another idea soon occurred to her that seemed worth following up.

While Hannah was fixing lunch, she called the film and theater critic of the River Heights newspaper. With the information that he provided, she was able to phone and talk to the producer of *Perfect Strangers* in New York. This was the Broadway play in which Clare Grant had expected to receive the leading role.

The producer, Barry Coe, was good-humored and accommodating. "Sure thing, Miss Drew. I'll be happy to see you this afternoon, if you can make it."

"Thank you, that's very kind. I'll be there," Nancy replied, elated.

As she was putting the phone down, Bess and George called to her from the front porch. "Hi,

Nancy! We've come to take you to lunch!"

Nancy laughed as she unlocked the screen door. "Sorry, Hannah's already got it on the stove. So come on in and join me."

"Okay, you've persuaded us," Bess said, wrinkling her nose and sniffing at the appetizing smell wafting from the kitchen.

George chuckled. "Me, too. I'll go along with that. Thanks, Nancy."

"Tell you what, let me put on that mysterious video cassette I told you about. You two can watch it while I'm setting the table."

Both girls wanted to help her, but Nancy overrode their protests. So while she set the table in the pleasant, sunny dining room and helped Hannah with the last-minute preparations, George and Bess watched the taped rock videos on the living room TV set.

Afterwards, over the hamburgers and salad at lunch, all three girls discussed the tape. But her two friends were as baffled as Nancy over why the cassette had been sent to her.

"It must have something to do with the lawsuit against Dallas Curry," Nancy mused aloud. "Otherwise, why was he sent all those video cassettes anonymously, too?"

"Speaking of Dallas Curry," George said, leaning forward, "what do you think, Nancy? Is he guilty or not?"

"I'm wondering the same thing," Bess murmured, taking a sip of her iced tea.

"Wow, that's a change in attitude!" Nancy remarked in surprise. "I thought you two were convinced of his innocence."

"Well, I guess we were," Bess admitted. "But today I'm not so sure."

"Neither am I," George chimed in. "He's certainly charming to listen to, but facts are facts. If he didn't copy those other people's ideas, how can you possibly explain his coming up with the same ideas?"

Nancy's two friends wanted her to come swimming with them at the country-club pool after lunch, but she begged off. "I've got an appointment in New York this afternoon with a Broadway producer," she told them with a smile.

"Nancy! Does this mean you've decided to go on the stage?" Bess squealed.

"Good heavens, no. I just want to talk to him about Clare Grant," Nancy replied.

"Oh," Bess said, deflated, at which George chuckled loudly.

"Any chance you two might care to join me?" Nancy went on with a hopeful glance from one girl to the other.

George shook her head regretfully and explained that she had promised to help out with

113

the lighting at a local rock concert that evening at Riverview College. Bess, however, was strongly tempted by Nancy's invitation.

"The only problem is," Bess said, gazing at her shorts and beach bag, "I'll have to change first."

"No problem," Nancy said and smiled. "We can stop at your house on the way to the airport."

With lunch over and the table cleared, the two girls picked up their tote bags of swimming gear and went out to the car with Nancy. Minutes later, she dropped George off at the country club, then headed for the Marvin house. It took Bess less time than usual to change clothes, an achievement she noted proudly.

Nancy grinned, but then an uneasy feeling settled over her, telling her that an important clue was staring her right in the face.

But what was it?

13

A Cute Cartoon

On landing in New York, the girls took a taxi to the theater where Nancy was to meet Broadway producer Barry Coe.

He proved to be as genial in person as he had sounded on the phone. He was in the midst of casting tryouts for his fall play, and was relaxing in a center-aisle seat when Nancy was escorted to him by one of his assistants. Much to her surprise, she learned that he had known nothing about Clare Grant's disappearance prior to her phone call.

"It's been on the television news, and I suppose in all the New York papers," said Nancy.

Barry Coe shrugged humorously and flung out his hands. "Just goes to show how ignorant I am. I took time out to get some sun down in the West Indies and just flew back the night before last. Since then, it's been nothing but conferences, phone calls, and tryouts. Anyhow, I'm intrigued. So tell me about it."

Nancy related the details of Clare's disappearance.

"That's certainly odd!" Coe frowned and shook his head. "I hardly know what to make of it."

"Do you know her well?" Nancy asked.

"Very well. I've known her ever since she appeared in *The Mandrake Root*. I directed that play, you know. Clare was fresh out of college then, a really talented young actress."

"I understand you were planning to give her the lead in your new play, *Perfect Strangers*."

Barry Coe looked surprised. "Where did you hear that?"

"From a friend of hers. Isn't it true?"

"Well, it's certainly not definite—in fact, I'd say it's not even probable. Clare's a fine actress, all right, but . . ." Coe broke off and rubbed his chin reflectively. "Well, I'm just not sure she's right for the part. Right now I'd have to say she only ranks as second or third choice for the leading role."

"Oh . . . " Nancy suddenly realized that this might account for Clare Grant's worried, anxious frame of mind that Pamela Kane sensed during their phone conversations. On the other hand, this would hardly explain the threats she had mentioned to Pamela.

When Nancy mentioned these to Barry Coe, he had no idea what Clare might have been referring to. On a sudden impulse, Nancy asked him if he was acquainted with Sylvia Salmo, Pamela's roommate who had recently come to New York.

"Sure, she and Clare came here together to break into show business," Coe recalled. "They were close friends—both stagestruck. But Sylvia was more into song and dance than acting. Her goal was musical comedy."

"Have you heard from her recently?"

"No, didn't even know she was here in New York. But if she is, and you're trying to find her, I can suggest a good place to look."

"I'd appreciate that," said Nancy.

"There's a new musical called *Moonglow* that's being cast right now," Barry Coe informed her. "If Sylvia's in town, it's a cinch she'll show up for the cattle call—you know, I mean the casting call, where dancers try out for the chorus line."

"How exactly could I find out?"

"Talk to Duane Weiss. He's the casting director for *Moonglow*." Coe took out a notepad and a pen and jotted something down, which he handed to Nancy. "There's his name and number. Give him a call and tell him I suggested you get in touch."

"I'll do that," Nancy said gratefully. "Thanks ever so much for your help, Mr. Coe."

"My pleasure, believe me."

As she was about to leave, the theatrical producer suddenly remarked, "By the way, did you ever see Clare Grant on stage?"

"No, I wish I had," Nancy replied. "I've just seen her photo a couple of times."

"Well, if you want to know what she's like, there's a caricature of her in Lilly's Restaurant. The walls there are covered with caricatures of actors and show-biz personalities. They put up one of Clare when she starred in *The Mandrake Root*. She had a cute way of tossing her head, something like this ... " Barry Coe struck a comical pose, which made Nancy and Bess laugh. "Take a look at that cartoon in Lilly's and you'll see what I mean."

"I will! And thanks again, Mr. Coe."

After leaving the theater, Nancy found a public phone in the lobby of a nearby office building. She tried to call Duane Weiss's number, but only got an answering service, whose operator was unable to tell her when Weiss might be available or where she might reach him.

Frustrated, Nancy hung up and debated her

next move. The thought occurred to her that if Sylvia Salmo had come to New York looking for work in show business, she would very likely have talked to a theatrical agent. Rather than waste the afternoon, she decided to go right down the list of such agents in the Yellow Pages telephone directory.

But after two calls, Nancy heaved a sigh. Each call was answered by a secretary who promptly lost all interest on learning that Nancy was neither a client nor producer. It was obvious that neither had the slightest intention of troubling herself to check out the name of Sylvia Salmo in the office files.

"Looks like I'll have to do this the hard way," she told Bess. After writing down a number of agents' names and addresses, whose offices were located within walking distance, she grinned. "How are your feet?" she asked her companion. "We have a lot of hiking to do."

"We do?" Bess said, wrinkling her nose in mock dismay. "Oh well, that's the price we have to pay for being good detectives." She giggled.

By the third fruitless office visit, however, Nancy had started to lose heart. So the girls stopped in a drugstore and Nancy made another try to reach Duane Weiss by phone—again with no luck.

Although the last thing on Nancy's mind was dinner, she couldn't sidestep Bess's sudden cheery reminder. "I'm getting hungry," she said. "Let's go somewhere really exciting to eat."

Nancy's face lit up immediately. "And I know just the place—Lilly's Restaurant!"

After finishing her round of visits to various theatrical agents, Nancy suggested the girls head for the restaurant. It was only a few minutes past six o'clock when they arrived. There were few diners at this early hour, but the visitors from River Heights found plenty to occupy their attention as they tried to identify the theatrical greats whose caricatures lined the walls.

Among them was the one of Clare Grant. It showed her with a big smile, tossing her head just as Barry Coe had described and mimicked, with one hand on her hip and the other hand fluffing up her hair at the nape of her neck.

"You know, Bess, it's funny," Nancy mused, "but I've a feeling I've seen her before—in person, I mean."

"Maybe you've seen her around somewhere, after she came to River Heights, but just didn't recognize her at the time," Bess suggested.

"That must be it."

After a delicious dinner and rich dessert, the

girls took time for a leisurely window-shopping stroll up Fifth Avenue. Then they took a taxi to the airport for the flight home.

As they got into Nancy's car, after landing in River Heights, Bess looked at her wristwatch. "We can still catch part of that rock concert, if you're interested, Nancy."

"Why not? . . . But let me call Dad first so he'll know where I am."

Although the group that was performing blared their music at a level that endangered the eardrums, the concert was lively and colorful, and Nancy enjoyed it thoroughly. From time to time, they caught glimpses of George. She was helping another girl manipulate the stage lighting for the benefit of the latter's boyfriend, who was video taping the concert.

Afterward Nancy and Bess met all three, and the young man who had done the video taping introduced them, in turn, to the members of the college rock group.

It was close to midnight when Nancy and Bess returned to Nancy's car in the parking lot. The teenage sleuth unlocked the passenger door for Bess, who then leaned over and unlocked the driver's door from the inside.

As Nancy opened it, there was a loud explosion!

14

Twinkling of an Eye

Both Nancy and Bess were shaken and stunned by the sudden blasting noise. A light had sparked inside the car when the door opened, and as Nancy recovered from the shock, she could see that her friend was still trembling with fright.

"Oh my g-g-goodness! Wh-What happened, Nancy?" she quavered. "D-Did the car blow up?"

"No, of course not, silly!" Nancy said, laughing in spite of her own fright. "If it had, we wouldn't be here talking to each other. But I guess we're okay, aren't we?"

Bess nodded, reduced to momentary speechlessness while she gulped and pulled herself together. "Y-Yes. At least we seem to be."

The explosion had brought people rushing to check on the cause, not only from elsewhere in the parking lot, but even from inside the college auditorium. Among the onlookers who gathered were George and the girl she had helped with the lighting and the latter's boyfriend, Peter Dornek.

"What in the world happened, Nancy?" George inquired anxiously.

"There was a loud noise when I opened the door—that's all I can tell you. Oh, oh! Wait a second." Nancy stooped down for a closer look as her keen eyes noticed something in the overhead light illuminating the parking lot. "There are some wires attached to the bottom of the door!"

Pete Dornek came forward and got down to peer and grope under the car. A moment later he held up some shredded fragments of a firecracker. "There's your answer. Some wise guy planted a cherry bomb under your car, along with a spark coil and battery. The way it was rigged, when you opened your door, the firecracker went off."

There was a ripple of nervous laughter and several joking remarks from the onlookers.

Nancy was not so amused but managed a good-humored smile. "Thanks, Pete. It's a relief to know that nobody was really trying to harm us."

As she drove out of the parking lot with Bess soon afterward, Nancy recalled the gas-station attendant's remark about how easy it was for an expert crook to break into a locked car. Perhaps a college prankster had just picked a car in the lot at random and planted a cherry bomb underneath to scare its owner after the concert. On the other hand, a more sinister plotter could have taken the opportunity to rig a much more deadly booby trap!

Was this someone's way of warning her not to go on investigating Clare Grant's disappearance or the mystery that had brought about the lawsuit against Dallas Curry?

Bess Marvin seemed to sense what was going on in the teenage sleuth's mind. "Was that firecracker just meant as a joke, Nancy?" she asked with a wide-eyed, anxious expression on her pretty face.

"That's exactly what I'm wondering, Bess." Then Nancy chuckled. "Whatever it was, I'd call it a lucky break!"

Bess stared in surprise. "Are you serious?"

"Yes, indeed. It's just given me the answer to

a question that's been bothering me all day!"

When Nancy started off for New York after lunch, she had been troubled by the feeling that an important clue was staring her in the face, which she couldn't quite identify. Now she knew what it was. The notion of a firecracker going off unexpectedly, when she was totally unaware that one had been planted under her car, had given her the idea of a different sort of booby trap altogether—this one *mental*!

For the moment, however, Nancy evaded Bess's further queries, preferring to wait until she had checked out her theory.

After breakfast the next morning, Nancy drove back to Ashton University for another interview with Professor Jaffee. He received her cordially in his private office.

"As I understand that experiment you were conducting yesterday," Nancy began, "you were trying to find out how much the students would remember of what they heard over their earphones while their conscious attention was aimed at the book they were reading."

Jaffee nodded. "That's right."

"And how much *did* they remember?"

"A surprising amount. The results of the experiment aren't all in yet, but when they were given a series of test questions about what they had heard, they all made high scores."

"That's amazing!" said Nancy, her eyes sparkling with interest. "Now tell me, Dr. Jaffee—is it possible to do the same thing by *sight*, rather than by *sound*? In other words, can an impression be made on a person's subconscious mind by what he takes in through his eyes, instead of through his ears?"

"Oh yes, of course. They're both examples of what we psychologists call subliminal perception."

The professor explained that the usual way of performing such an experiment visually was to flash an image on a movie screen for a mere split-second. This might be done while the person was watching a movie. The interruption would occur at such lightning speed that the person would not even be aware it had happened. Nevertheless, his subconscious mind would still remember that fleeting image.

"I must add that the whole subject is very much up in the air," Jaffee went on with a dry chuckle. "Some psychologists don't even like to talk about it, because it raises so many troublesome questions. For instance, governments could use subliminal perception for propaganda purposes, to influence public opinion.

And, of course, advertisers could use it to make people want to buy whatever they're trying to sell. So advertising agencies get very upset about it, too. They're afraid if the public starts worrying about subliminal perception, people might get angry and suspicious about all sorts of advertising."

Nancy nodded thoughtfully and explained what had brought her to the professor's office. First she told him about the mysterious video cassette that had been sent to her anonymously. "After I had watched the tape on our television set, I found myself disliking Dallas Curry before I had even met him . . . and I was willing to believe he was guilty of copying other people's work without even waiting to hear all the facts."

Her two girl friends' attitudes, Nancy continued, had been just the opposite. They had started out by liking Dallas Curry and believing he was innocent.

"But after they viewed the tape yesterday, their opinion changed. They, too, began thinking he might be guilty. Could all this be due to subliminal perception, caused by something on the video tape?"

Dr. Jaffee nodded emphatically. "Yes, from what you tell me, I would say that's quite possible."

"And could Dallas Curry have been . . . well, let's say, 'programmed' to copy someone else's advertising layouts the same way—I mean, by subliminal perception?"

Jaffee frowned and tugged at his lower lip. "That's a bit more difficult to answer. But if skillfully done, I would say yes—that, too, is possible. Why do you ask?"

"Because some unknown person sent *him* video cassettes in the mail, too!"

After leaving the professor's office, Nancy stopped at a public phone on the campus and called George Fayne. "Do you suppose that friend who video taped the rock concert last night would be willing to do me a favor?" Nancy asked.

"Don't be silly, of course he would," said George. "Why?"

"I'd like him to slow down that video tape you and Bess saw at my house and examine it, frame by frame. Could he do that?"

"Sure, I imagine so. He works in the college's TV studio. They have all kinds of recording equipment there."

"Good! And I might ask him to do the same thing with those tapes Dallas Curry received in the mail."

"Okay. I'll call Pete and let him know you're

coming," George said. "He's probably at the studio right now, editing that tape he shot of the concert."

"Thanks a million," Nancy said and hung up. As she headed for her car, her spirits were soaring. Before she left Jaffee's office, the professor had promised to gather some written information about subliminal perception and send it to her to read. And, with luck, she might have the suspicious video tapes analyzed before the end of the day.

Nancy's heart beat faster with the elated feeling that the solution to at least one of her two mystery cases was now within reach!

15

A Question of Dates

Nancy steered deftly into her driveway, jumped out of her car, and walked into the house with a light step. The sooner she delivered those mystery tapes to Pete Dornek at the college TV studio, the sooner she could hope to find out if her hunch was correct—and right now her hunch felt stronger than ever!

"Home to stay for a while, dear?" Hannah Gruen said and smiled from the kitchen doorway, wiping her hands on her apron.

"Not really, Hannah. I have a couple of errands to run, so don't bother fixing me anything to eat . . . thanks just the same."

Nancy picked up the music video cassette from a table in the living room and put it in her shoulder bag. Then, going to the hall phone, she dialed Dallas Curry's number.

"Hi, this is Nancy Drew," she said when the famed photographer answered in person. "Do you suppose I might borrow those mysterious rock video cassettes you played for my friends and me the other evening?"

"You most certainly may."

"Oh, fine! Would it be convenient if I picked them up right away?"

"More than convenient. You could do me a big favor by having lunch with me," Dallas Curry declared. "I'm getting awfully tired of my own company. Takashi's trying to cheer me up. He tells me he has a special treat for lunch."

Nancy chuckled. "It sounds too good to turn down, so I accept."

The tanned, handsome photographer came out to greet her as she parked in the driveway of his spacious, wooded estate fifteen minutes later. He was wearing a silk sports shirt open at the neck and white duck boating slacks. "Nancy, you don't know how happy I am to see you!"

Despite, or perhaps because of, his cheery manner, Nancy sensed that her call had caught him in a depressed mood. "It's nice to be here and see how lovely your place looks in the daylight," she responded.

"Yes, it is beautiful, isn't it," he murmured proudly, gazing about at the house itself and the surrounding sweep of emerald lawn and trees. "And because it's such a great day outside, we're going to eat on the patio."

"Wonderful!"

Offering Nancy his arm, Dallas Curry conducted her along a shady, flagstoned path, which wound among the trees and shrubbery, only to emerge again at the rear of the house into bright sunshine, with banks of flowers on each side of the walk.

"Oh, how fragrant!" Nancy breathed. "Are you a gardener as well as a photographer?"

"Not yet . . . but I may turn into one, if I don't win this lawsuit and clear my reputation. There might be nothing else for me to do!"

"Let's keep our fingers crossed then and hope you do win!" Nancy was tempted to tell him all about her new and promising lead, but cautiously decided to say nothing until she knew whether or not the results would bear out her hunch.

Meanwhile, Curry opened the door to a screened-in patio, where comfortable chairs and sofas invited one to laze about. In one corner, a table had been set with sparkling silver and glasses. "Goodness, that makes me hungry to look at, even before the food's been served," Nancy observed with a smile.

"You'll be even hungrier, I trust, when it is. Takashi's quite a wizard in the kitchen." Curry helped Nancy to a chair, then sat down himself. "Tak's as happy as I am that you've come to lunch, by the way. He claims I've been moping around in solitary too long."

The white-jacketed houseman soon appeared, bowing and smiling, and proceeded to serve a delicious Japanese-style meal of steak and seafood. Nancy found herself eating with a hearty appetite and enjoying every morsel.

It was evident from Dallas Curry's remarks that the unpleasant accusations of copying, and the lawsuit brought against him by the Marc Joplin agency, had caused a sudden halt to his professional assignments. Not only was he receiving no more phone calls from magazines and ad agencies—even friends and acquaintances, it seemed, had dropped him out of embarrassment over the stolen layout scandal.

As the meal progressed, however, Curry grew more cheerful, thanks to Nancy's lively and sympathetic efforts at conversation. Even after lunch was over, he did his best to delay Nancy's departure by showing her some of his most famous photos, which were mounted on walls all over the house.

Among them, along with war scenes from his days as a news photographer and glowing fashion shots in full color, were several enlarged photos from his magazine picture story on Clare Grant when she was a typical, stagestruck youngster who had not yet won Broadway fame. One intriguing photograph showed Clare posed dramatically on what looked like the parapet of a castle tower.

"Where was that taken?" Nancy asked. "In England?"

Dallas Curry smiled. "No, in Westchester County, New York. It's what's called an architectural 'folly.' Know what that means?"

"Well, let me see . . . an odd-looking building that's probably quite useless?"

"Precisely! Rich people sometimes built them just for fun, a century or two ago—mostly in England or Europe, but there are a few over here, too. Some were designed to look like old Greek or Roman ruins. This one looks like part of a fake medieval castle."

"It must be quite a sight," Nancy commented.

"Yes, charming place. It was used as a

straw-hat theater at the time this was taken."

Suddenly Nancy snapped her fingers. "That reminds me of something, Mr. Curry, that I've been meaning to ask you."

"Sure. And call me Dallas, please, not Mr. Curry," he said, smiling.

"Okay," Nancy said and smiled back. "I assume most of your advertising layouts are photographed in ... well, sort of in secrecy, aren't they?"

The photographer nodded. "As far as possible. Every agency and its clients try to keep their new advertising campaigns confidential before they're launched."

"Then where did that torn-up photograph of your Statue of Liberty layout come from—the one that I told you was found in the woods behind the Fyfe house?"

Dallas Curry frowned and rubbed his jaw thoughtfully. "Wait—yes, I remember now. I sent Clare herself a copy. I thought it might make quite a nice addition to her modeling portfolio."

"And did Clare mingle socially with any advertising people at that time?" Nancy went on. "Or perhaps date any advertising executives?"

"Oh, sure. She'd often show up at agency parties. She didn't have any acting jobs just then, you see, so she had to rely on modeling assignments for her bread and butter."

"Then that could be a way that someone in the advertising business got a look at your Statue of Liberty layout long before it was published," Nancy exclaimed. "I mean that person might have visited Clare, or come to pick her up for a date, and seen that photograph you sent her!"

Curry's eyes widened. He was obviously startled by Nancy's suggestion. "By George, I never even thought of that!"

"Can you remember her dating anyone from one of those agencies you're in trouble with?" Nancy asked.

There was a long silence. Dallas Curry frowned, then shook his head in exasperation. "You know, Nancy, I believe I do recall seeing her with someone like that, but I just can't remember who he was."

Nancy waited hopefully, but in vain. Curry gave up at last with a hopeless shrug. "No use. Whoever it was, his name or face just doesn't come to me."

"Well, keep trying, and if you do remember who he was, please let me know." She added with a smile, "And now I really must be on my way, Dallas. Thanks ever so much to you and

Takashi for that delicious lunch."

Dallas Curry proceeded to collect the various video cassettes that he had received anonymously. Nancy put them in her shoulder bag and, after saying good-bye, went out to her car.

She was just about to drive off when he came hurrying out to join her.

"I've just remembered Clare's date!" he exclaimed. "I'm sure I saw her once or twice with a fellow named Ted Yates!"

Nancy felt a surge of excitement as the name registered in her memory. Ted Yates was one of the persons she had met at the Stratton Agency!

16

A Trio of Suspects

"Thanks, Dallas," Nancy said. "That information may be important!"

With a wave, she started down the drive, hopefully mulling over what she had just learned. When she had visited the Stratton Agency, the firm's receptionist had first referred her to the account executive who had prepared the Knights of the Round Table ad for their furniture-manufacturer client. This executive, who proved to be a small, dark, fashionably dressed man named Ted Yates, had told Nancy almost at once that it would be best if she talked directly to the firm's president, Mr. John Stratton.

Perhaps, Nancy now mused, Yates had been

anxious to avoid talking to her for fear she might know about his acquaintance with Clare Grant.

When Nancy got to Riverview College, she parked in the lot where the cherry bomb had exploded the night before. A student directed her to the college's TV studio. She found Pete Dornek ensconced in a workroom of the studio, surrounded by monitor screens and the optical and electronic equipment that he used in editing his tape of last night's rock concert.

"Have any more hidden firecrackers gone off?" he inquired with a grin.

"None since that one you discovered under my car, thank goodness." Nancy chuckled. "As a matter of fact, I need your help again, if you can spare the time."

"You mean to check out those mysterious video tapes George mentioned on the phone? Sure, I'd be glad to. What exactly am I supposed to look for?"

"Anything that doesn't seem to belong on the tapes. They're a series of music videos—as George may have told you—but I've a feeling something else may have been inserted here and there, maybe something that would appear on the screen for a fleeting instant." Nancy explained what she had just learned about subliminal perception from Professor Jaffee.

Pete Dornek nodded. "Yes, I've heard about that sort of thing being done, but I've never run across an actual example. What you're asking me to do should be quite interesting, Nancy. I'll get on it right away."

Nancy thanked him and went back to her car. Her mind was already busy on the next step in her investigation. If the video tapes had indeed been doctored in the way she suspected, it could mean only one thing—that someone had deliberately tried to frame Dallas Curry and ruin his professional reputation. But *who* . . . ?

As Nancy drove away from Riverview College, she decided that the best place to search for the culprit might well be one of the three ad agencies that claimed Dallas Curry was guilty of copying layouts.

And I may as well start by checking out Ted Yates, she mused. If he had dated Clare Grant, he might easily have seen her copy of the Statue of Liberty photo—the layout that had started all the trouble. And as account executive for the Stratton Agency's furniture client, he must have been involved from the very first in preparing that Knights of the Round Table ad—the second copied layout.

Almost without pausing to make a conscious decision, Nancy found herself driving out to

Possum Road instead of going straight home. There was only one person who might be able to tell her something about Clare Grant's acquaintance with Ted Yates, and that was Pamela Kane.

Nancy parked in the driveway of the Fyfes' white chateau and rang the bell. Pamela Kane, eager for news, opened the door and led her into the living room. But when Nancy brought up the name of Ted Yates, Pamela almost scornfully rejected the notion that he and Clare had ever been romantically involved.

"But Dallas Curry says he saw them together," Nancy pointed out.

"That doesn't prove they dated. At a party, Clare may have talked to lots of people," Pam argued. She paused and frowned reminiscently, then shook her head. "No, honestly, Nancy, Clare and I kept in close touch by phone—sometimes we'd have long chats at night—and if she'd been dating this Ted Yates fellow, I'm sure I would have heard about him. But I never once remember her mentioning that name."

"Whom did she date, then?" Nancy asked. "Are there any definite names you remember?"

"There certainly is—one at least!" Pamela declared. "In fact, I was going to phone you, if you hadn't stopped by just now."

The blonde, pixie-bespectacled young woman said that ever since finding Oliver Snell's phone number among Clare Grant's personal effects yesterday, she had been racking her brain, trying to remember why Snell's name seemed so important to her. "And then it came to me, Nancy—that name just suddenly clicked in my memory! They must have been quite close at one time."

Nancy gazed keenly at her informant. "What makes you think so, Pamela?"

"Because they were dating steadily for a while! I definitely remember Clare telling me so and talking about him. Besides, why else would she have his number? It's the only one I found among Clare's things."

Nancy pinched her lower lip thoughtfully. "You may be right. I certainly intend to follow up and find out more about him, Pam."

Nancy left the Fyfes' house with a definite plan of action in mind. She would begin her search for the guilty party by concentrating, for the time being, on the likeliest suspect at each of the three advertising agencies.

And I'm going to check up on Ted Yates, no matter what Pam says, Nancy decided. If she had forgotten or overlooked Oliver Snell's name until his phone number turned up among

Clare Grant's personal effects, how could Pamela be sure that Ted Yates's name hadn't also slipped her mind? At any rate, Dallas Curry definitely remembered seeing him with Clare, and that was enough for Nancy to go on at this point.

Arriving home, she settled herself in a comfortable chair by the living room telephone extension and placed a call to the Stratton Agency in New York. "Mr. John Stratton, please," she said when the firm's operator answered.

The next voice on the line was that of Stratton's secretary. "May I ask what your call is in reference to?" she inquired loftily.

"The photographer, Dallas Curry, and the charge that he copied one of your agency's advertising layouts."

Stratton sounded somewhat gruff when Nancy was finally put through to him. "I thought we covered all this ground when you came to see us on Tuesday, Miss Drew."

"I appreciate your time and courtesy in talking to me, Mr. Stratton," the teenage sleuth said politely. "But some new information has come up that makes me think it would be worthwhile to know more about each of the layouts that Dallas Curry is accused of copying. In the case of that Knights of the Round Table furniture ad, Mr. Ted Yates was in charge of preparing the layout, is that right?"

After a pause, Stratton replied with a curt yes.

"Then could you tell me something about Mr. Yates, please."

There was another pause. Then Stratton said, "Miss Drew, I've already told you that a copy of that layout was stolen by someone who broke into my agency. The break-in was definitely an outside job, and no one in the firm had anything to do with it. I'm certain of that. Therefore, I see no reason to discuss Mr. Yates with you, especially since our charge of ethical misconduct is already under review by the Advertising Council. If you'll excuse me now, I'm a busy man." With a curt good-bye, he hung up.

Nancy heaved a rueful sigh and pressed the cut-off button to get another dial tone. Her plan of attack was off to a limping start and had just run into a blank wall. Nevertheless, she proceeded to dial the New York number of Marc Joplin, Inc.

Unhappily, this call met with an even colder response. Not only did the president of the agency refuse to tell Nancy anything about Oliver Snell, his attitude was downright hostile. When she tried to convince him that her only interest was in finding out the truth about the mysteriously copied layouts, the executive snapped, "The fact remains, Miss Drew, your father is the opposing counsel in our pending lawsuit. The proper place to settle this dispute is now in a court of law—and that's precisely what we intend to do. Good-bye."

Undeterred, Nancy phoned the third advertising agency, Darby & Wallace, which was actually the first one she had called on in New York. The firm's executive vice-president, Mr. Knapp, was as polite and open as he had been on Tuesday. Nancy was grateful for this, even though she realized this might be at least partly due to his regret and embarrassment over Rick Hyatt's unpleasant behavior.

"How can I help you, Miss Drew?" he asked.

Nancy explained, as she had done on her two previous calls, that she was trying to find out more about the copied layouts and the person who had created them.

"Meaning, in our case, Roscoe Leff?" Mr. Knapp inquired.

"Yes, sir. Has he always worked for Darby & Wallace since he entered the advertising business?"

"Yes . . . well, that is, except for one short period a couple of years ago," Knapp corrected himself. "He left briefly to try and start up an agency of his own, but it didn't work out."

"What happened?" Nancy asked.

"Well, he had high hopes of landing the Murdo Chemical account. That one account would have earned him a sizable profit and put his agency into the big time in one fell swoop . . . but unfortunately it didn't work out. So he soon came and asked for his job back with us," Knapp explained.

"I see." Nancy asked him several more questions, then thanked him and said good-bye. Frowning thoughtfully, she put down the phone. What she had learned from her calls was very little. Still, any lead was worth following up.

Her train of thought was interrupted as she heard someone rapping on the front screen door. Then George Fayne's voice called out excitedly:

"Hey, Nancy! . . . Wait'll you hear the news!"

17

Secret Images

Nancy hurried to let her friend in. "What's up, George?" she asked.

"Plenty! I just had a call from Pete Dornek, and he says your hunch was right, Nancy!"

"Something was inserted in the video tapes?"

"Yes. He's already spotted about half a dozen weird frames that have nothing to do with the rock videos, and he's not even through analyzing the tapes."

Nancy proposed eagerly, "Can we go and have a look at what he's found?"

"I was afraid you'd never ask," George said with a chuckle. "Let's go!"

The two girls hopped into Nancy's car, which

was soon whizzing toward Riverview College.

Pete Dornek greeted them as they came into the TV studio and led them to his workroom. "I've taken all the inserted frames that I've discovered so far," he explained, "and recorded them on a separate tape. I think they may give you quite a shock, Nancy."

He flicked several switches and dials on his complicated control board and pointed to one of the monitor screens. Both Nancy and George gasped at the lettering that appeared on the screen:

DALLAS CURRY IS A CHEAT AND A THIEF!

Again Pete flicked a switch and a new frame appeared. This one said:

DALLAS CURRY STEALS OTHER PEOPLE'S IDEAS!

A moment later, he switched to still another frame:

CURRY IS GUILTY—GUILTY—G U I L T Y ! !

Nancy's heart beat faster. Even though she had expected the tapes to reveal something like this, now that the evidence was vividly on display before her very eyes, she found herself almost breathless with indignation and anger. "This is really mean and contemptible!" she exclaimed. "What a vicious, underhanded way to ruin someone's good name!"

The thought that her own opinion of Dallas

Curry had been influenced in this way made Nancy even more upset.

George heartily agreed. "Whoever did this is sick!" the dark-haired girl declared.

"Well, that's not all," said Pete Dornek, "although the frames you've just seen are the most shocking. All those, by the way, were inserted in the video tape *you* received, Nancy—and there are probably more that I haven't spotted yet. But the inserts are totally different in the cassettes you got from Curry. Those are both pictorial. I don't even understand them, but you probably will."

He now showed a picture of knights in armor seated at a round table—the second advertising layout that Dallas Curry was accused of copying.

"About eight or nine frames just like this were inserted in one of the tapes," Pete commented.

Then he flicked a switch to show another frame on the monitor screen—this one portraying models' faces superimposed on flower blossoms in a garden. This was the layout that had brought on the lawsuit.

"I found this picture cropping up again and again in another of Curry's tapes," said Pete.

Nancy sighed and shook her head. "I can still

hardly believe it, but this certainly makes it clear how Dallas Curry got into trouble."

For example, after Curry played the first video cassette repeatedly, Nancy explained to Pete and George, the Knights of the Round Table image would be deeply imprinted in his subconscious mind. "So if he were assigned to create an ad for a furniture manufacturer," she went on, "this is the idea that would naturally occur to him!"

The same method had been used to trick him into copying the cosmetics layout with the models' faces superimposed over flower blossoms.

"Do you think this evidence will be enough to clear him?" George Fayne asked excitedly.

"I hope so," Nancy replied. "Dad will be able to answer that question better than I can, of course. But I'm not going to stop there, anyhow, George. I intend to find out who's responsible for this whole mean, heartless plot!"

Pete Dornek by now was thoroughly caught up in the excitement of Nancy's mystery case. He promised to finish analyzing the suspicious tapes even before he went back to editing his own tape of last night's rock concert.

"The job takes time," he added. "I have to play over each tape, bit by bit, in slow motion and then freeze-frame each insert so I can re-cord it on a separate tape. But I should be done by tonight."

"Thanks ever so much, Pete," said Nancy. "Your help is really important in cracking this case!"

George had a tennis date with her boyfriend, Burt Eddleton, at four-thirty that afternoon, so Nancy dropped her off at the Faynes' house before returning home. After parking in the driveway a few minutes later, Nancy was surprised to find Pamela Kane waiting in the living room.

"Hi, Pam!" the titian-haired teenager greeted her. "This is certainly a pleasant surprise. Have you turned up a new lead on Clare's disappearance?"

"No, but I've been doing a lot of thinking, Nancy, since we talked earlier this afternoon. I'm more convinced than ever that Oliver Snell is involved somehow!"

Nancy stood facing her blonde visitor and pondered her emphatic remark. "And you base this on the strength of what you've already told me—that he and Clare dated, and you found his number among her things?"

"Isn't that enough?" asked Pamela. "Who else do we know who's more likely to have been in touch with her just before she vanished?"

Nancy nodded slowly and mused aloud, "Yes, you may be right about that." In any case, she had already decided that she would have to return to New York if she hoped to find out who—if anyone—at the three advertising agencies was behind the plot to frame Dallas Curry.

Now, it seemed, Pamela was pressing for an immediate confrontation with Oliver Snell. "What exactly do you have in mind?" Nancy asked her.

"I'd like to meet him and talk to him as soon as possible. Could you possibly arrange for the three of us to have lunch?"

Again Nancy nodded, after a moment's thought. "Yes, perhaps. At any rate, there's no harm in trying."

"Then please try, Nancy!"

"Very well." Nancy went over and sat down by the living room phone, and proceeded to dial Oliver Snell's direct office number, which Pamela had brought along in her purse.

When Snell answered and heard Nancy Drew's voice at the other end of the line, his manner became frigid. "Mr. Joplin has told me about your call earlier this afternoon, Miss Drew. Surely you understand why I'd better

154

cut this conversation short right now and hang up."

"Yes, I do understand, Mr. Snell," she said calmly. "But something new has come up, which may be very important—and in all fairness, I think you should have a chance to tell us your side of it."

"Who is 'us'?"

"A young lady named Pamela Kane. It appears that you and she have a mutual friend."

"And who might that be?"

"I think I would prefer to let Miss Kane tell you that herself," Nancy replied. "Are you free for lunch tomorrow, Mr. Snell?"

There was a brief, strained silence. Nancy could sense his conflicting emotions, even over the phone, with curiosity warring against suspicion and resentment. In the end, curiosity won out. "All right," he said sullenly. "Where would you like to meet?"

"Any place that you think would be convenient and suitable, Mr. Snell. After all, you know the restaurants in midtown Manhattan better than I do."

"Hmph. Very well." Snell named a restaurant, suggested they meet at twelve-thirty, and hung up curtly.

Nancy put down the phone and turned to Pamela with a smile. "All set," she said.

"Terrific, Nancy!" Pamela said and beamed.

By the time Carson Drew arrived home that evening, Nancy had had a further report on the video tapes from Pete Dornek. He said he had found more insert frames like those he had already shown Nancy and George, but no photos of the Statue of Liberty layout. Nancy told her father the encouraging news.

"That's amazing, my dear! It's the best news I've had since Dallas Curry asked me to take his case!" Mr. Drew enthused. "In fact, if we can persuade Professor Jaffee to testify about subliminal perception as an expert witness, this might just be enough to win the lawsuit. Of course, our case would be even stronger if we knew who was behind the plot."

"That's the next thing I'm working on, Dad." Nancy told him what she had learned from the president of Darby & Wallace about Roscoe Leff's unsuccessful attempt to win the advertising account of Murdo Chemical. "It's not much of a lead, but it's a chance to find out more about Leff. You've handled several legal assignments for the Murdo Chemical Corporation, haven't you, Dad?"

"Yes, their main plant's just over in Hillport,

you know, and the head of the company often lunches here in River Heights. That's how I came to meet him in the first place."

"Could you arrange for me to meet him?" Nancy asked.

"Hmm ... yes, I can certainly try, dear ... though it goes without saying that he's a very busy man."

Nancy was content to leave it at that, knowing that Carson Drew's legal services were highly valued by all his clients. She felt sure that the head of the Murdo Chemical Corporation would do his best to oblige the distinguished attorney.

Meanwhile, tomorrow's lunch with Oliver Snell might prove highly interesting!

The next morning, as Nancy was eating breakfast, she heard Hannah Gruen chatting with the mailman at the front door. A few moments later, the kindly housekeeper came into the dining room with the morning mail.

"Anything for me, Hannah?" Nancy asked over the rim of her coffee cup.

"Yes indeed, dear ... a rather important-looking package!"

18

A Pair of Enemies

Nancy eagerly took the package from Hannah. It was a sealed, manila envelope, and she guessed its contents at once after seeing the sender's name in one corner: PROF. H. JAFFEE, PSYCHOLOGY DEPT., ASHTON UNIVERSITY.

Her guess was confirmed when she opened the envelope and read the note inside.

> *Dear Miss Drew:*
>
> *Here is the material on subliminal perception that I promised to dig up for you. I trust you'll find it interesting and helpful, but if you need any*

*more information, please don't hesi-
tate to call on me.*

> *Sincerely yours,*
> *Hugh Jaffee*

The note was clipped to a number of techni-
cal articles about subliminal perception, obviously photocopied from various professional
journals.

Nancy was sure she would find them interesting and looked forward to reading them. They
might be just what was needed to clinch Dallas
Curry's innocence in the minds of a judge and
jury.

But at the moment, Nancy had little or no
time to spare. She was due to pick up Pamela
Kane at the Fyfes' house on Possum Road soon
after breakfast and then drive to the River
Heights airport. The two had arranged to take a
short commuter flight to New York City.

"By the way, I'll be gone overnight, Hannah," Nancy said as she set down her coffee cup
and dabbed her lips with a napkin.

"Oh dear, we'll miss you," Hannah said,
pausing on the way to the kitchen. She was trying hard not to sound like a worried parent, although Nancy knew that the motherly housekeeper always did worry when she was away
overnight.

"I shan't be alone," Nancy said, bobbing up from her chair to give the housekeeper a fond hug. "I'll be going with Pamela Kane, so we'll be able to keep an eye on each other."

"Where will you be staying, dear? With your Aunt Eloise?"

"Probably not. Pam said she'd make reservations for us, so I'll phone from New York and let you and Dad know."

"Be sure you do, now—please, Nancy!"

"I promise, Hannah."

Nancy scampered upstairs to shower and dress. Half an hour later, after slipping a few things into an overnight bag, she left the house with a final kiss and wave to Hannah Gruen.

By eleven that morning, she and Pamela Kane were ensconced at the Drury Lane, a small, inexpensive hotel in the heart of Manhattan's theater district, where Pamela had evidently stayed before. While her companion freshened up and reapplied her makeup, Nancy phoned home to River Heights to tell Hannah where they had registered.

Forty minutes later, the two were embarking by taxi for the restaurant that Oliver Snell had named. The midtown traffic was heavy as always at this time of day. Even so, it was not yet twelve-fifteen when they reached the restaurant.

Somewhat to Nancy's surprise, Snell had already arrived and was waiting for them at a secluded corner table. He rose to greet them with a curious glance at her companion.

"Pamela, this is Mr. Oliver Snell," Nancy introduced them, then murmured in turn to the agency art director, "Miss Pamela Kane. She's from California and is visiting here in the East."

"I see," said Snell as they shook hands. He added when they were seated, "I understand that you and I have a mutual friend, Miss Kane."

"That's right," Pamela said with a challenging smile. "Clare Grant."

A look of astonishment passed over Snell's face. "The young actress who disappeared!" As he spoke, his astonished look changed to an expression that Nancy couldn't decipher. Was it puzzlement or relief, or possibly just one of wary interest?

Nancy said, "Pamela tells me that you and Miss Grant were quite friendly at one time."

Oliver Snell frowned. "I've taken her to dinner once or twice, if that's what you mean."

"Clare and I are old friends," Pamela remarked. "In fact, we shared an apartment for a while in Los Angeles. After Clare came back East, we kept in touch and had long phone chats two or three times a week. She often

161

talked about you, Mr. Snell . . . and from what she said, I certainly got the impression that you had many more dates than just taking her out to dinner once or twice."

Pamela spoke in an almost accusatory tone, and Snell's face took on an irritable flush. "On one of those dinner dates, Miss Kane, I took Clare to a Broadway show. Another time, we attended an agency party and ended up having dinner together. If we had any more dates than those two occasions, I don't even remember them."

The conversation was interrupted as a waiter came to take their orders. Afterward, Nancy tried to ease the tension by changing the subject and chatting about lighter topics, such as current Broadway plays she had read about, and one that Ned Nickerson had taken her to see at a matinee performance.

Later, as they began eating lunch, when she felt that Snell was sufficiently relaxed and off guard, Nancy said suddenly, "Have you ever seen that Statue of Liberty fashion ad that Dallas Curry is accused of copying from a Darby & Wallace layout?"

Snell seemed to stiffen and darted a suspicious glance at the titian-haired teenager. "Of course I've seen it. By this time, so has every other ad man in New York. It's what started this whole scandalous mess that Curry's gotten himself into. What about it?"

"Are you aware," Nancy asked, "that Clare Grant was the model who posed for Mr. Curry's version of that layout?"

"Naturally," snapped Oliver Snell. "Since I knew Clare and had taken her out a couple of times, as I just got through telling you, I could hardly *help* recognizing her."

"Did you know that Dallas Curry sent her a copy of that photograph soon after he took it?"

"No, I didn't know that. Why on earth should I?" Snell asked defensively.

Nancy shrugged. "If you dated Clare twice, you might have come to pick her up. And if she had that layout photo lying around loose in her apartment, you might have seen it."

Oliver Snell glared at the young sleuth. "So that's why you organized this lunch! Let me tell you, Miss Drew, that I was *never* in Clare Grant's place. She lived down in the East Village part of the city—at the opposite end of Manhattan from me. That time I took her to a Broadway show, we met at the restaurant after work, so we could dine early with no rush and have plenty of time to make the opening curtain. On the other occasion, we met at the agency party and went out to a restaurant from there. That's how we first became acquainted, in fact."

Pamela Kane shook her head dubiously, as if unconvinced. "That certainly isn't the way it sounded when Clare described your relationship to me. As I told you, she spoke as if you'd had a number of dates."

"I can't help how she spoke to you," Snell retorted in an exasperated voice. "I'm telling you the facts."

"If you never came to Clare's apartment," Pamela persisted, "how did you know it was in the East Village?"

"Because she told me so, that's how." Snell turned his glance angrily on Nancy. "And let me add, Miss Drew, that if I *had* seen that Statue of Liberty photograph, it wouldn't have meant the slightest thing to me. Neither I nor the agency I work for had anything to do with that layout, then or later."

"So you say, Mr. Snell," Pamela remarked with a cool smile. "But the fact remains that that layout is about to figure in a sensational lawsuit. And Clare Grant, who posed for that layout, has disappeared. You seem to be the one connecting link between those two cases. Has that fact ever occurred to you?"

Oliver Snell looked both furious and badly shaken at the same time. He opened his mouth as if to explode angrily, then closed it again. "Think what you please, Miss Kane," he snapped. "And that goes for you too, Miss Drew."

The atmosphere throughout the rest of the meal was strained and awkward. To Nancy's surprise, Pamela now changed her tone and began to chat almost flirtatiously with the agency art director. Snell, too, seemed startled and puzzled by her different manner. At one point, Nancy noticed him staring at the young blonde-haired woman.

As the lunch drew to a close, Snell gulped down his coffee and rose abruptly without waiting for the two girls to finish their desserts. Pulling out his wallet, he slapped down some money on the table.

"That should cover the bill and tip. If you'll excuse me now, I have to be getting back to the office," he said and stalked out of the restaurant.

Nancy sighed and looked at Pamela with a rueful smile. "Well, was it worthwhile? Did we learn anything from this luncheon?"

Pamela shrugged airily. "I think we stirred him up a good deal, don't you? And when we tell the police and the news media what I just told Mr. Snell, I rather imagine it'll stir things up a lot more!"

"You intend to give an interview on the subject?" Nancy inquired in surprise.

"Certainly, why not? But I think the place to begin is at the New York Police Department."

"I'm sure the River Heights police have already been in touch with the New York police about Clare's disappearance," Nancy pointed out mildly.

"Maybe so," said Pamela. "But I'm sure I can get more action by going to New York City Police Headquarters in person—and that may just include some action against our friend, Oliver Snell. He should at least be *questioned* by the police, if you ask me!"

Unfortunately, however, Pamela had spilled some ice cream on her dress. So she decided to return to the hotel first before starting downtown to police headquarters.

While she was changing, their room phone rang. Nancy answered and heard her father's voice.

"How are things going in New York, dear?" Carson Drew inquired.

Nancy chuckled dryly. "I think I'd better wait to answer that question until the investigation's

166

farther along, Daddy. What's up at your end of the line?"

"Well, this is rather short notice, Nancy, but I've just arranged an interview for you with Eli Jaxon, the head of Murdo Chemical Corporation. There's just one hitch."

"What's that?"

"He'll be glad to talk to you, but it'll have to be this afternoon, if you hope to see him at all. He's about to leave for Europe."

"Oh, dear!" Nancy was caught completely by surprise. "I—I'm not sure I can manage that."

"If you're worried about getting here, that's no problem. Murdo Chemical Corporation has a company helicopter, which happens to be at La Guardia Airport in New York right now, picking up an emergency repair part for their plant. If you could get out there in the next hour, Mr. Jaxon says you can fly here in the helicopter and then return to New York with him in their company jet. He'll be leaving the plant around four-thirty."

"That's certainly generous of him! Let me think it over for just a moment, Daddy."

Was the interview worth such an abrupt change in plans? Nancy pondered quickly. Slim as it was, she had had a hunch from the very first that her lead on Roscoe Leff was worth

167

following up. She also realized that she was not looking forward to accompanying Pamela Kane to the police headquarters in New York City. If Pamela's behavior toward Oliver Snell at lunch was anything to go by, her talk to the local police officials to goad them into stronger action was likely to be rather melodramatic!

Nancy was not even sure that the results were likely to be very useful. In any case, Pamela was certainly capable of dealing with the police on her own, with no help from Nancy.

"Okay, Daddy," she decided. "Please tell Mr. Jaxon that I'll accept his invitation gratefully."

Pamela looked annoyed when she heard about Nancy's change of plans and tried to talk her out of returning to River Heights. But Nancy, having made her decision, was a firm-minded young lady. She promised to rejoin Pamela later that afternoon, and was soon on her way to La Guardia Airport.

The company helicopter landed at the Murdo Chemical Corporation plant, and she was escorted at once to Eli Jaxon's office.

The bald, heavyset industrialist was a shrewd, friendly looking man. He invited Nancy to be seated and asked how he could help her.

"I was told," Nancy began, "that a couple of

years ago, a man named Roscoe Leff formed a new advertising agency and tried to win your company's advertising business."

Jaxon nodded. "Yes, that's so. Leff wasn't working by himself, however. He formed his agency in partnership with another man."

"Really?" Nancy was surprised. "I didn't know that. Do you remember who the other man was?"

"Hmm, let me see. His name will come back to me in a moment." Jaxon frowned thoughtfully and drummed his fingers on his desk. "Shell, or something like that. No—Snell, that's it! Oliver Snell."

Nancy's eyes widened. "But they failed to land your account?"

"True. Mind you, they submitted a proposal for a new advertising campaign that made a very favorable impression, both on me and my board of directors."

"What exactly happened?" Nancy inquired.

"Well, several other agencies were also competing for our business and submitted proposals, too. One of them came up with an ad campaign that sounded every bit as good as the one dreamed up by Leff and Snell. We couldn't make up our minds about which to choose."

"So how did you decide between them, Mr. Jaxon?"

"We called in a famous photographer, Dallas Curry, and asked his opinion. He lives in River Heights, perhaps you know him. He's a law client of your father's, I understand—also an old friend of mine who once photographed our plant, in fact. He favored the other agency's proposal, so Leff and Snell lost out."

Nancy stared at the chemical company president, for a moment almost too startled to speak. What Mr. Jaxon had just told her meant that Dallas Curry had—not one—but *two* potential enemies!

Obviously both had good reason to want revenge on the famed photographer. By causing Eli Jaxon and Murdo Chemical's board of directors to pick the other ad agency instead of theirs, he had spoiled their chance to form a successful new business of their own.

But who—either Oliver Snell or Roscoe Leff—had masterminded the sinister plot to ruin Dallas Curry's professional reputation?

19

The Unsigned Message

Nancy thanked Mr. Jaxon for his help, her brain still busily working away at the mental jigsaw puzzle. She felt surer than ever now that she was nearing a solution to at least one of the two mysteries.

Meanwhile, Nancy reflected with a sigh, she had promised to return to New York. When she had first agreed to stay overnight in the city, it had been in response to Pamela Kane's urging that they engage in some joint sleuthing there for clues to Clare Grant's disappearance. At the time, this fitted in very well with Nancy's plan to investigate the three main agency suspects in the Dallas Curry case.

But now, sensing that a solution was close at hand to the latter mystery, Nancy was less inclined to spend time on any generalized search for clues. For the moment, she wanted to concentrate on finding out who had tried to frame Dallas Curry.

Still, she couldn't leave Pamela stranded in New York City.

Mr. Jaxon arranged to have an aide from the company's public relations department take Nancy on a brief sightseeing tour of the plant while he was winding up his work for the afternoon. But first she decided to call home on a public phone in the plant lobby, in order to tell Hannah her plans.

"Then there's a chance you may come back home tonight, after all?" the housekeeper inquired.

"I hope so, Hannah, if I can persuade Pamela Kane."

"By the way, George is here, dear. We were just chatting in the hallway when the phone rang."

A sudden thought struck Nancy. "Oh gosh, Hannah, would you let me speak to her? Maybe she'd like to come back to New York with me—that is, if there's room aboard, and Mr. Jaxon won't think I'm too forward in asking!"

As it turned out, George was delighted at the idea. And Mr. Jaxon readily assented to taking Nancy's friend along on the flight.

"Glad to, my dear," Mr. Jaxon said with a jovial smile when Nancy made her diffident request. "There's plenty of room for another passenger in our company's executive jet."

George was waiting eagerly at the Murdo Chemical Corporation hangar when he and Nancy arrived at the airport in the helicopter. The jet was already fueled and standing by for takeoff. After a short, pleasant flight, it touched down at La Guardia Airport in New York. From there, a taxi whisked Nancy and George into Manhattan. The afternoon was drawing to a close when the two girls walked into the lobby of the Drury Lane Hotel. Nancy picked up the key from the desk clerk, and they went up to the room.

Pamela Kane was not there. "She was bound and determined to get the NYPD into the act," Nancy said with a rueful grin. "It wouldn't surprise me if she was down at headquarters right now, nagging the police commissioner to do something!"

Nancy kicked off her shoes, thinking they might as well make use of the time while they waited for Pamela.

"Make yourself comfortable, George," she said aloud. "I have a phone call to make."

Sitting down on the edge of one of the beds, Nancy fished in her shoulder bag for a moment.

Then she picked up the room phone, asked the operator for an outside line, and dialed the number of Duane Weiss, the casting director of the upcoming musical, *Moonglow*.

This time she was in luck. Weiss not only answered the phone himself, he recognized Sylvia Salmo's name instantly. "Sure, we've already signed her up for the chorus line," he said cheerfully. "Hang on a sec. I'll give you her phone number and address."

As usual when investigating a mystery, Nancy preferred a face-to-face meeting, rather than a phone conversation, and now seemed as good a time as any. So the two River Heights girls took a taxi to Sylvia's apartment, which was not far away on the East Side.

The young woman who opened the door to the apartment left Nancy momentarily speechless with surprise. Though slightly taller than Pamela Kane, Sylvia Salmo, too, had long blonde hair and pearl-rimmed pixie glasses!

She seemed rather startled herself—almost unpleasantly so, Nancy thought—on hearing the reason for the teenage sleuth's visit.

"What more can I tell you?" she said and shrugged. "Pam knows Clare Grant a lot better than I do." She did not even invite her two visitors to sit down, explaining that she had to get ready for an evening date.

"Not very friendly, was she?" Nancy commented quietly as they walked out of Sylvia's apartment building into the street.

"You said it," George agreed.

"I'm getting hungry," Nancy said impulsively. "How about you?"

"Ditto!"

"How about Lilly's? They have a caricature of Clare Grant up on the wall there, and I'd like another look at it. Would you like to eat there?"

"I'd love to," George exclaimed. "Bess told me all about it, including that cartoon."

Nancy paused as they passed a phone booth. "Wait till I try the hotel again. Pamela may want to come with us, if she's back."

The young detective hung up and emerged from the booth a few moments later with a shake of her head. "Still no answer from the room," she reported. "Oh well, come on. Let's go."

It was somewhat early for the New York dinner crowd, and the two girls found few diners in the restaurant when they arrived. So when Nancy requested a table near the Clare Grant caricature, the headwaiter willingly obliged.

George stared at it, after their orders had been taken. "It's really cute," she remarked. "So is Clare Grant, if that's a good likeness."

"It is, according to the director of that stage play she was hoping to be in," Nancy replied. She broke off suddenly, recalling the astonished look that had come over Oliver Snell's face at one point during lunch.

A wild idea had just taken shape in Nancy's mind. But at the moment, it seemed too far out to explain to George. Better think it over and check it out a bit first, she decided.

Less than an hour had passed by the time the two girls finished their coffee and dessert. "Pam surely ought to be back by now," Nancy remarked as they left Lilly's and began briskly walking the few blocks to the hotel.

But Pam was not there. When Nancy asked at the desk, she was handed the room key and informed that Miss Kane had come in about half an hour ago—only to find a phone message waiting that had caused her to go out again.

Nancy sighed and turned to George. "We may as well wait for her upstairs. No telling how long she'll be gone."

They went up from the lobby by elevator and then relaxed in the room. George sat down to watch television. Nancy brightened as she recalled the manila envelope that had come in the morning mail. Now was her chance to read that material on subliminal perception that Professor Jaffee had sent her!

She pulled the envelope out of her overnight bag and extracted the articles. Then she settled herself in an easy chair, with her stockinged feet propped up on the bed, and began to read.

Because of the devious trick played on Dallas Curry and herself, Nancy found the photocopied material intensely interesting. She raced through the first article, then the second. When she came to the third article, Nancy froze in surprise and stared at the name of its author. *The piece had been written by Oliver Snell of the Marc Joplin advertising agency!*

Her thoughts were in a whirl. Not only did Snell have a strong motive for revenge on Dallas Curry—he also had an expert knowledge of subliminal perception!

She recalled how Pamela Kane had reported finding his phone number among Clare Grant's personal effects—the mysterious threats to Clare that Pam had been so concerned about—and the accusing way she had harped at Oliver Snell during lunch.

And suddenly Nancy knew for sure, with a sinking heart, why he had stared at Pamela in such open-mouthed astonishment!

She sprang up from the chair and laid the manila envelope and articles aside. "Be right back, George. I'm just going down to the lobby," Nancy called as she went out the door.

George looked away from the TV set and nodded.

In the lobby, Nancy walked straight to the reception counter and asked about the phone message that Pamela had found waiting for her when she returned to the hotel. "Did you notice what she did with it after she read it?" Nancy asked the clerk.

He frowned and shrugged. "Just crumpled it up, I think, and threw it away."

"Where?"

"Right over there in that ashtray. In fact, I think I can see it from here . . . that yellow slip of paper."

Nancy hurried to retrieve it and smoothed out the wrinkles enough to read the message:

MISS KANE—BE AT THE TOWER AT 8:00 TO-NIGHT AND I WILL GIVE YOU SENSA-TIONAL EVIDENCE IN THE CLARE GRANT CASE. BUT COME ALONE OR IT'S NO DEAL!

"Incidentally," the desk clerk added, "she arranged to rent a car before she left."

"I'd like to rent one, too," Nancy said, making a lightning decision. "Could you order one for me?"

"Sure thing, Miss Drew. I can have one brought right to the door of the hotel in ten or fifteen minutes. And the rental agreement will be all made out for you to sign when it gets here."

Nancy thanked him and hurried back up to the room, her heart pounding. After consulting the address book in her shoulder bag, she picked up the room phone, asked for an outside line, and dialed Dallas Curry's number.

"Oh, thank goodness you're home!" she blurted out when the photographer answered. "I can't explain now, Dallas, but I need to know the exact location of that tower in Westchester County . . . the one you showed me, where you took that photograph of Clare Grant. You said the building used to be a straw-hat theater."

She listened intently for a few moments, then said, "Thanks, Dallas—I'll tell you all about it later!"

Nancy turned to her companion, who by now was staring at her questioningly, startled by Nancy's anxious manner and tone of voice.

"George, we have to leave here right now and get going fast! I'm afraid Pamela Kane may be in danger!"

20

Tower of Danger

Luckily the rush hour was past, but traffic was still fairly heavy on the expressway leading north from Manhattan through the Bronx and up into Westchester County.

As she drove, Nancy explained her theory to George, who at first was so surprised she could hardly believe what her friend was telling her. "You can't be serious, Nancy?" she gasped.

"You bet I am, George. It's the only possible answer!"

Nancy debated stopping at a roadside phone to alert the police to Pamela Kane's danger. But a glance at her wristwatch frightened her. Time was running out, and every minute might be precious! Then she thought of the time it might take to get through to the right police jurisdiction, followed by the problem of identifying herself and convincing the police operator that her call was neither a youthful prank nor a case of hysteria!

Part of the problem was that her story sounded so wildly improbable, and the explanation of her theory even more so. Even George had had difficulty in taking her seriously!

In the end, Nancy stayed in her seat and kept on the road, her fingers gripping the wheel tightly and her foot pressing down on the accelerator as hard as she dared.

Her tension communicated itself to George, and the last dozen miles or so of the trip sped by in fearful silence, both girls sitting stiffly upright with their hearts thudding.

The castlelike architectural "folly" that Dallas Curry had described to her lay well beyond the outskirts of the nearest small town. Dusk was gathering as the tower itself loomed into view. Nancy's pulse skipped a beat as she glimpsed two figures swaying on the parapet. They appeared to be either embracing or struggling!

Nancy braked to a halt, flung open her door, and leaped out. George nimbly did the same!

As they raced toward a shallow flight of steps and a heavy, oaken door in the front wall of the castle, George cried, "What if it's locked?"

"It can't be!" Nancy shouted back. "*They* got in!"

Sure enough, it opened on their first try. Inside, beyond a flagstoned vestibule, lay the gloomy, balconied great hall of the castle.

"Over there!" George exclaimed, pointing to a circular flight of stone stairs in one corner, which wound upward into darkness.

Nancy reached it first, with George close at her heels. To light their way, Nancy switched on a flashlight, which she had snatched from the car's glove compartment, almost without thinking, before jumping out.

Panting for breath, their hearts pounding, the girls came to an overhead trap door. They pushed it open and scrambled on through to the roof of the tower.

A few yards away, Oliver Snell was locked in a struggle with Pamela Kane. His one hand was clamped to her throat, while his other sought to push her backward over the brink of the parapet! Despite their difference in size and strength, Pamela fought back fiercely. But her glasses and blonde wig had come loose, and the hand squeezing her throat had cut off her cries for help.

Nancy and George darted to her rescue. Nancy hit Snell over the head with her flashlight as hard as she could. As he started to crumple from the blow, George hooked an arm around his throat and dragged him backward.

Pamela collapsed into Nancy's arms. Her lips were trembling and she struggled for breath. Not only her pearl-rimmed pixie glasses but her blonde wig were completely off now, exposing her own pinned-up dark hair underneath.

"There, there, it's all over," Nancy murmured soothingly. "You're safe now, Clare!"

Much later that same night, Nancy stood facing a number of people in her own living room at home. Among them were Carson Drew and Hannah Gruen, her friends Bess and George, Police Chief McGinnis, and Dallas Curry.

The girl detective had just finished describing Clare Grant's elaborate scheme to "disappear" and assume the identity of a visiting friend from California with the made-up name of Pamela Kane.

Nancy explained how, in the early hours of darkness on Monday morning, Clare had

crawled out her bedroom window at the Fyfes' house with her appearance disguised, and then had borrowed a bicycle from the garage and ridden to the gas station down the road.

There she had loaded her bike onto the station's pickup truck and driven back via Possum Road to the cinder path toward the woods. By *backing* from the path toward the quarry and returning to it by the same method, she made it appear that the vehicle had approached from and driven off in the direction of Highway 19. While at the quarry, she had also returned the bicycle to the garage and scattered her torn-up photograph through the woods so as to lead searchers toward the quarry. The man's footprints that were found must have been made some other time, probably by a fisherman.

"But how was she able to get the gas-station truck started in the first place?" Bess asked.

"She had made a soap impression of the extra key during an earlier visit to the station," Nancy explained.

After returning the pickup truck to the gas station, Nancy continued, Clare had gone to the bus depot in town, where she later hailed a cab to the airport. She had retrieved a suitcase that she had earlier stashed in a rental locker.

In the ladies' room, Clare took a blonde wig, glasses, and a change of clothes from the suitcase and donned her new disguise as Pamela Kane, before starting off in a cab to the Fyfes' house.

"But hold on, dear," Mr. Drew said with a frown. "I thought my private investigators found out she'd flown here from California."

"That was her friend, Sylvia Salmo," said Nancy. "Meanwhile, their other roommate back in California was all primed to answer any questions detectives might ask."

She added, "That ether can under the window, by the way, was planted by Clare-alias-Pamela early the next morning, in order to try to convince me she'd been kidnapped."

"All clear so far," said Dallas Curry. "But now tell us about this plot by Oliver Snell to ruin my reputation."

"It all started when he dated Clare one evening and saw the photograph of your Statue of Liberty layout. He passed a sketch of it to his pal, Roscoe Leff, who copied it for a fashion layout of his own and made sure it got published before yours."

This mean trick tickled Snell so much, Nancy explained, that he decided to repeat it and wreck his hated enemy's career. Having heard that Ted Yates was working on a furniture ad, Snell hired a street hoodlum to break into the Stratton Agency and steal it. Then he inserted images of this layout in a rock-music video tape and sent it to Curry anonymously, followed soon afterward by another tape of the same sort. As an expert in subliminal perception, he was confident that this would implant the image deeply enough in Curry's subconscious mind so that Curry would eventually use the same image to "create" an identical layout of his own.

"And later on," said Nancy, "Snell dreamed up the cosmetic flower-face layout, and again used the same trick to make it appear as if Dallas had stolen his idea."

She added that Snell had also had the same hoodlum trail her and plant the cherry bomb under her car as a warning to get off the case. He had also filched several parts from her CB radio at the same time, to keep her from ever calling the police while he was trailing her. Snell was now under arrest in Westchester County, and the hoodlum was being hunted by the police in New York City.

There was still more to Clare Grant's story,

however. "She suspected that Oliver Snell had seen the photo of the Statue of Liberty layout at her flat and was behind the plot to ruin Dallas Curry. So she did her best to tie her own fake disappearance in with the lawsuit against him, which she was sure would get plenty of TV coverage."

"But why on earth would a talented young actress do such a thing, Nancy?" asked Hannah.

"I'm afraid it was a rather pathetic attempt to clinch the leading role in a new play. She had the mistaken idea that if she got her name in the headlines, the director would be more eager to hire her for the part. Eventually she planned to reappear and pretend she had suffered temporary amnesia, which would prevent the police from proving she had disappeared on purpose."

George Fayne grinned faintly. "You still haven't told them how you guessed who Pamela really was."

Nancy smiled back. "It was the cute way Clare Grant had of turning her head slightly and smiling in a flirtatious way out of the corner of her mouth. Only Oliver Snell wasn't amused. He decided he would have to stop her from exposing his own plot."

For a moment, Nancy wondered if her next

mystery would prove to be as dangerous. She would find out when she solved *The Emerald-Eyed Cat Mystery*.

"But you outguessed him just in time," said Bess, interrupting Nancy's thought. "Same old story—*Nancy Drew to the rescue*—ta-daaah!"